NOT QUITE A DUCHESS

THE BOSTON HEIRESSES BOOK 1

AVA ROSE

CONTENTS

CHAPTER ONE

WREXFORD HOUSE, BOSTON

October 1891

"Do you know if His Royal Highness, Prince Penforth, will be in attendance tonight, Your Grace?" Edith Harper asked as she accepted a glass of lemonade from a passing footman.

Anna rolled her eyes at Edith's formal address. Saying she disliked being called *your grace* would be putting it mildly. Yes, Anna Trevallyn was now a duchess in her own right and the daughter of one of England's most influential dukes, the late Duke Wrexford, but she would rather be called Anna. Or

Lady Anna, if one insisted on formality. She had made that clear to everyone in her circle since the day her father received the rare permission to pass the coveted title down to his daughter. Edith, however, was the obsequious type and always used formal address.

"I don't know," Anna answered, glancing around. *Would* Penforth attend? He usually did, but then locked himself away somewhere private seemingly to avoid everyone. The prince was an enigma that Anna had not yet managed to solve.

Edith turned and tapped the shoulder of their companion, Elizabeth Armstrong-Leeds. Libby was far more agreeable than her enigmatic brother, and had been Anna's best friend for many years. "Will your brother be in attendance tonight, Your Highness?"

Libby, whose debate with Lord Remington had just been interrupted, huffed out an annoyed breath. "How would *I* know?"

"Oh, but why not? He *is* your brother."

"I hardly know what is in my brother's mind," she replied with an impatient air, before turning her attention back to Lord Remington.

Edith ignored the obvious rebuff and turned back to Anna. "How does my dress look?" She smoothed the skirt of her pink satin evening dress.

Anna's eyes did a slow assessment of the woman's appearance. The dress was too colorful for the current moment, when women preferred the sophistication that blues and greens gave them. The mint green flowers on the dress did nothing to beautify the garment. If anything, the whole ensemble clashed with Edith's pale complexion.

"Pretty as a cake," Anna lied, plastering on a false smile as she scanned the guests. She loved hosting parties like this, but they could veer toward the tedious when proper conversation was lacking, and ladies like Edith Harper often talked nonsense.

"Lady Anna," Lord Remington called her attention. "Since you love to discuss politics, who do you think will win the coming mayoral race for our fair city of Boston?"

Anna sighed before replying with a stiff smile, "I hardly think this is the place to discuss such matters, sir."

He scoffed, "You are afraid, you mean?"

Anna raised a brow. Ever since she'd shown awareness of any subject other than painting, sewing or looking for a husband, men challenged her just to prove their own superiority and remind her that, as a female, her opinions were worthless.

"Sir, I am loathe to discuss the topic in a crowded ballroom. As the hostess of tonight's soiree, it is my duty to ensure everyone has an enjoyable time."

He tugged down his vest and pushed his chin forward, ready to engage. "I rather think——"

"Please excuse me, I think my attention is required elsewhere." She cut him off, leaving him standing with his mouth opening and closing like a washed-up fish. *Not a good look, my Lord.*

As she swiveled away from Remington, Anna collided with someone. She didn't need to look up to know who it was. She could feel his strong energy shrouding her, pulling her into its mysterious depths. Firm hands shot out to steady her.

"You need to watch your step," came his deep voice, finally drawing her gaze up to his.

His Royal Highness, Prince Penforth Armstrong-Leeds' dark eyes arrested hers, trapping them in a hard stare that sent a slight shiver through her body. As always, he unsettled her. She could not understand why she always reacted to him so strongly. He was not a nice man, and neither was he in possession of any particular charm.

Penforth was a hundredth or so in line for the throne of the tiny principality of Eskoania, but he was still a prince nevertheless. A Baron, too. Though one could hardly discern his ties to senior peerage unless advised of them.

"Penforth," she said, trying to sound insouciant. He released her immediately, bowing slightly in greeting.

"Your Highness, how wonderful to see you!" Edith came up to them, offering her gloved hand for a kiss.

Anna mentally rolled her eyes. The woman must have been anticipating this moment since her arrival.

To his credit, Penforth placed a soft kiss on Edith's knuckles and murmured, "Likewise," before giving Anna a glance of dismay.

She grinned at him, suddenly enjoying herself, and his brows came down.

"I would have been most disappointed had you not turned up tonight," Edith simpered.

"I am sure," he said brusquely, his obsidian gaze still on Anna.

Save me, those eyes pleaded. At least, that was what Anna imagined. The prince would never plead with anyone, but it was evident he wanted to get away from Edith. With an impertinent wink and a smile she hoped was suggestive, she slipped away, but not before her ears caught his frustrated groan. For once, Edith had done something good for Anna; rescued her from having to suffer the company of such a man.

As expected with any gathering of Boston's finest, there was a confounding need for everyone to converse with the hostess. Anna had graciously taken it upon herself to play that role while her widowed mother was staying with family in England, and Pen watched with growing frustration as Anna was accosted at every turn by either a society matron seeking to match her with a son who had just come into his title, or a gentleman aiming to challenge her views on worldly matters. Or even worse, in Pen's view—wanting a dance.

It seemed as if everyone wanted a piece of the unusual Duchess Wrexford. It wasn't often an unmarried woman inherited a title such as hers. It was testament to the strength of Anna's personality that Boston society had not turned their backs on her for the controversial decision by her late father, but rather, had stepped up their efforts to ingratiate themselves.

It annoyed the devil out of him that there did not ever seem to be a spare minute in which he could talk with his sister's greatest friend.

"There are people out on the terrace. Shall we step out for some fresh air, Your Highness?" Miss Harper asked, squeezing his arm.

He'd almost forgotten her existence. "I would rather remain indoors. It looks like a storm is coming," he replied, still keeping his eyes on Anna. She was dancing now with a gentleman he did not recognize.

There were very few moments in which he wished his injury did not impair his ability to dance…this was one of them. He did not like Anna Trevallyn—he hardly liked anyone—but she moved with so much grace he felt the urge to be the one holding her, twirling her, having those lovely blue eyes gaze up into his.

"Oh, you don't like storms?"

"On the contrary."

"Then why don't you want to go out onto the terrace?"

He tore his eyes away from Anna long enough to study Miss Harper's face. "I do not wish to get wet. Would you like another drink?"

Her green eyes glittered as she breathed a hearty, "Oh, yes! Perhaps, champagne this time?"

Pen steered the woman toward the refreshment table where he picked up a fresh glass and handed it to her. After she'd taken several sips, he pulled her hand out from the crook of his elbow and gave it an avuncular pat.

"It was nice seeing you, Miss Harper. Please excuse me." He turned and left.

"What about the terrace?" she called after him.

Pen ignored her. He should feel guilty for abandoning her like that, but his conscience had long since been squelched into non-existence. He had little patience for women who were not his mother or sisters, and even less for women such as the simpering Miss Harper.

His mood was already dark; add the dull pain in his leg to the mix and the beast within began to stir. Exiting the ballroom, he made his way to the room where he often spent time while at Anna's social events—the empty salon down the hall. He poured himself a glass of the fine brandy that sat on a sideboard.

Much more suitable to his mood than lemonade or insipid bubbles.

"Remind me again why I attend these dratted parties," he muttered out loud.

The answer hovered in his mind but he would rather be shot than admit the truth.

AFTER A WALTZ THAT HAD FELT INFERNALLY LONG, Anna gratefully accepted a glass of lemonade from a passing footman. She had just taken a sip when she heard her name called. She turned to see Libby approaching.

"Look." Libby pouted and pointed down at her emerald-green dress. The front, from the middle of the bodice right down the skirt, was soaked.

"What happened?"

"Edith happened," Libby ground out. "I don't know why I tolerate that stupid woman."

Anna's head swiveled to look for Edith. She found her standing by the refreshment table, looking forlorn.

"Didn't I leave her with Pen?" Anna asked.

Libby rolled her eyes. "You know my brother. He dumped her over there, and in her distress she poured champagne all over me."

Anna huffed out a breath. "What a waste of fine silk. Though I am sure she didn't do it on purpose."

"I know. I am just very irritated right now. I'll go upstairs and change."

Libby was staying with Anna while the latter's mother was away. Not that she was much of a chaperone. The two friends were as bad as each other when it came to adventure. Even though Libby lived only a short distance away, they had half-lived in each other's homes since the moment they first met.

"Feel free to grab one of my dresses," Anna called as Libby left to change.

She looked out the window briefly before she was asked to dance again. It was windy and the overcast night sky foreshadowed a storm. Out of the corner of her eye, she caught a footman—one of the newly hired ones—exiting the ballroom with several full glasses of champagne on a tray. It was quite unusual for that many full glasses to be taken out when nearly all the guests were either in the ballroom or on the terrace which extended from the ballroom, but she decided not to worry about such things tonight.

By the hour of midnight, Anna's head was spinning and there was a harrowing storm outside that none of the guests seemed concerned about. If one more gentleman asked her to dance, she was going to faint. Well, her robust constitution would not exactly permit her body to swoon, so she would have to feign it.

Looking once more at the rain-pelted windows, a chill went through her, causing her to wrap her arms around herself. The storm did not look like it would let up any time soon. If anything, the rain and wind appeared to be increasing. The almost deafening sound of thunder made her jump.

Then seconds later, everything went dark.

*P*en blinked in the darkness, willing his eyes to adjust before he moved from his chair. Presumably the storm had somehow caused damage to the new-fangled gas lighting system. There was something to be said for the old ways. A candle and sconce could always be relied upon. He remembered seeing a taper and a matchbox on the escritoire by the window somewhere to his left and, feeling around, he found and lit the taper. He made his way back to the ballroom intending to find his sister and check on her welfare before heading home. Surely all the guests would now wish to depart, and perhaps he could beat the crowd and leave before the roads became too congested with carriages.

He found chaos where before, order had

reigned. The music had stopped, and the ballroom exits were choked with everyone trying to get out all at once. Pen could feel their collective panic thickening the air. It was just a blackout, and candles had been relit and still illuminated the hallways of Wrexford House. He could not understand their panic. That said, he could not understand why the Boston Brahmins did half the things they did.

After what seemed like a long wait, the ballroom doors cleared enough for him to pass through. He looked around for Libby but could not see her. He looked for Anna next and found her talking to an elderly matron. Again, he had to wait, this time for the old lady to finish complaining about how wet it would be outside.

"Have you seen Libby?" he brusquely asked, as soon as the lady was out of earshot.

She looked around the room, a frown of concentration stilling her usually animated face. "I think she must still be upstairs in her room. Her dress was ruined earlier and she went up to change. I don't think she's come back down."

"She's probably tired," he surmised. "Tell her good night from me. I'm heading home shortly."

A wry smile lifted the corner of her mouth and

her vivid blue eyes gleamed in the candlelight. "You do have it in you, after all, don't you?"

He immediately put up his defenses. "What do you mean?" If he let her, Anna would pick him apart sinew by sinew.

"You can be sweet when you want to be."

"Yes, well, Libby *is* my sister."

"I suppose that doesn't count, then."

"Have you finished nattering? I must leave."

When most women would have been outraged by his deliberate crassness, Anna only looked amused.

"I take back my statement, sir," she said. "Perhaps you are not sweet at all."

"It's the reason we never talk. Besides, I have no obligation to be nice to anyone."

She quirked a brow. "You wanted to see Libby and bid her goodnight before you leave. That is not nice. Not nice at all!"

"She is my *sister*," he ground out.

She grinned. "Exactly my point."

The little minx had just twisted the situation around and made him inadvertently admit things. "Goodnight," he said and swiftly turned on his heels without so much as a bow.

As much as she loved baiting Penforth, it was time to put him out of her thoughts. What had happened to Libby? It was unlike her to not return to the ballroom after changing. Pen might be right and she was tired, but she'd not looked it. The more Anna thought about it, the more an unsettling feeling found its way to her stomach. It was unexplainable, but something did not feel right.

She took a lit candlestick from a side table in the hallway and went upstairs. It might be nothing. It also might be the storm, or the darkness, or even the champagne she'd had, that was causing this feeling of dread to settle deep within her bones.

With tentative hands, Anna opened the door and stepped into the room. The wind hit her first, blowing out the candle in her grip, and her arm came up to shield her face. She put the candlestick down on the carpeted floor and went to pull the shutters closed. Once done, she turned to look around the darkened room, not quite seeing anything clearly.

"Libby?" she called, quietly at first.

Silence was the only answer.

"Libby, are you in here?"

The faint dread that had foreshadowed this moment came back with full intensity. Trying not to panic, Anna found a match and relit the room's candles before searching the area and adjoining chamber for her friend.

Everywhere was empty. Yes, the princess had obviously been here, because her ruined dress lay on the bed.

But Libby herself was missing.

PEN PULLED A GOLD WATCH FROM HIS VEST POCKET and checked the time. So much for beating the crowd. There was a long line at the front door with most guests reluctant to step out into the rain. He'd been waiting for a quarter of an hour for the entrance to clear. Sadly, things had only gotten worse with the gaggle of ladies dominating the area insisting on waiting until the rain let up.

Had they failed to recognize that this was a storm? One that certainly did not look like it would be subsiding anytime soon. There was a simple solution that no one seemed to be thinking about.

He stepped forward, cleared his throat, and said in a clear, loud voice, "Ladies and gentlemen, it isn't safe to journey to your homes in these stormy conditions. Perhaps if we all return to the ballroom, I am positive Lady Anna will see to our comfort."

"Oh, what a splendid notion," he heard a

gentleman call out from the back. There was a rush of murmurs as the guests agreed. Then in a very civilized manner, the crowd began a procession back toward the ballroom.

Pen was about to look for Anna to confirm his suggestion when a hand grasped his sleeve. He turned to find the very person he was seeking, worry etched on every fine contour of her face.

"What is the matter?" he quickly asked.

She pulled him aside, into an alcove. "Libby is not in her room. I have searched everywhere on the second floor to no avail."

Something stirred in his chest, something quite like fear.

"We'll find her," he said firmly. "I trust you don't mind, but I've sent the guests back to the ballroom to wait out the worst of this weather."

"Not at all," she confirmed. "I should have thought of that myself. I was so focused on looking for Libby…"

Anna appeared calm, but from the set of her mouth and the straightness of her back, he knew there must be worry stirring within her.

"Would you like me to arrange a small search party? I can liaise with your butler. Webb, isn't it?"

"Yes, certainly Webb can assist. But, should we

both attend the ballroom first, so as not to arouse curiosity?"

Anna's suggestion was a sound one. He hadn't thought to keep things hushed until she mentioned it. Now that she had, concern for his sister's welfare grew. Where the devil had Libby disappeared to?

The ballroom was surprisingly calm. The duchess's staff had managed to light the various sconces and there was a pleasant glow permeating the space. As though they could sense that something was amiss, the guests' attention turned to Anna when she stepped up to address them.

"This storm certainly is playing with us this night, is it not?" Despite the situation, her joking manner did the trick, defusing tension. They all laughed.

"Prince Penforth is right to suggest you stay. It is not safe for the carriages and horses, and certainly not any of you out there. Please make yourselves comfortable. I have three drawing rooms and a salon at your disposal, and I will have tea and further refreshments brought in shortly."

Some murmured their thanks while others complained. One could never please everyone, Pen mused, even though their host's generosity could not be faulted.

Anna disappeared then, and he lingered in the ballroom for a short stint before following behind. He found her in the kitchen, speaking to the housekeeper and making arrangements for the guests.

Her efficiency was admirable. Within minutes, she had arrangements under control; the previously panicked guests were placated by the promise of food and comfort, and a quiet search for Libby was already underway.

Between Anna, Webb, and himself, they made a surreptitious but thorough sweep of the ground and upper floors. There was no sign of his sister. With every minute that passed, his fear grew. She couldn't have left the house in a storm such as the one now raging outside…she was not that insensible. The only explanation he could think of was that she had been removed against her will.

Kidnapping. His stomach lurched at the thought.

They went back upstairs to her rooms. At first glance, nothing seemed out of the ordinary, but the longer Pen stood in the middle of the bedchamber and observed, the more he realized that the space looked as if it had been left in haste. The dress Libby had been wearing at the ball was thrown haphazardly on the bed, her jewelry box open with a string of pearls dangling over the edge, and her silver hairbrush was on the floor by the foot of the vanity table.

Yes, she could very well have left the room in that state in her hurry to rejoin the party, but she was not at the party now. So where in the devil *was* she?

Her draped cloak on the chest at the foot of the large mahogany four-poster bed stood out. If Libby had indeed left the house voluntarily, she would have surely taken her cloak with her. There was always the possibility that she had taken a different cloak, perhaps one of Anna's, although that seemed unlikely.

"How long ago did she retire to change?" he asked Anna.

"Just after ten."

He cursed, mostly under his breath, disregarding Anna's presence and sensibilities.

Pen moved to the window, his shoes making a squishy sound when he stepped on the carpet near the window. It was soaking wet. The windowsill was also wet, as was the nearby escritoire and the items atop it.

"Was this window closed when you first came in?"

"No, *I* closed it." Anna moved to sit on the bed. "It was already windy when she came up. She wouldn't leave the window open knowing it was about to rain." The sound of thunder crashing made her wince. "This is all my fault, Pen. I should have been paying closer attention."

"Don't blame yourself, Anna. We are not sure yet what has happened, or why."

She shook her head. "No, I disagree. I think we do know what has happened." Her blue eyes met his. "Someone took her, and from my home, no less. There's no other explanation that fits."

Pen did not want to think. He only wanted to act, to find his sister and bring her back to safety.

"We'll find her," he vowed. "I'll go and search my house. I am not sure it will be helpful, but I have to start somewhere and it is always possible she chose to leave early, prior to the storm, and head home to bed."

Anna stood. "I'll come with—"

His hands shot out to stop her. "It's past midnight and there is a storm. You are not going anywhere."

"But—"

"No." His tone brokered no argument and she clamped her mouth shut. "Stay here and make sure no one finds out what is going on. Libby's reputation is at stake already."

"I *know* that," she replied with an edge to her voice.

Pen turned and headed for the door. "Keep everything in this room as it is," he called over his shoulder.

"And if she's not at home?"

He paused on the way out. "If she is neither here, nor there, then I see no alternative but to contact the police department."

CHAPTER THREE

*W*hen Anna awoke in the morning with a cramp in her neck from sleeping awkwardly in a chair, she wished last night's events had all been a dream. The guests had finally left well after one and Anna had sat in the drawing room, feeling at a loss and trying to come to grips with what might have happened until five when sleep stole in.

She glanced at the clock on the fireplace mantle. Seven o'clock. She scrambled to her feet and ran upstairs, calling for her lady's maid as she went.

"Eva, help me get dressed, quickly," she said when her maid entered. She tugged impatiently at the laces of her corset.

Once her clothing and undergarments were out of the way, she splashed some water on her face and cleaned herself before being cinched into a new corset and stepping into a midnight blue velvet dress. She then pulled on her sturdiest boots. It was cold outside and Anna had no intention of sitting around waiting for someone else to do something.

"You're not going to eat anything, my lady?" Eva asked when Anna threw on her cloak and made for the massive oak front door.

"No, I have urgent business."

The walk to the Armstrong-Leeds house seemed to take forever despite the short distance and Anna's quick steps. The streets were littered with leaves and debris from last night's winds, and a thick fog swirled all around her, clouding visibility. If one were in mourning, the gloom of the day would weigh heavily. Anna was no longer in mourning for her father, who had passed more than three years earlier, but the gloom still got to her, too.

Her friend was missing and there were no leads to follow.

I will find you, Libby. She was determined on that point. If the reverse were the case, she knew Libby would not rest until Anna was found and the perpetrators brought to justice.

She couldn't begin to fathom a life without her friend. In fact, Libby was not just a friend; not having any siblings of her own, Anna saw a sister in the other woman. They shared everything, from their world views about everyone's right to vote, to a pact to remain spinsters for the rest of their lives unless the right man swept in to claim their heart with true love.

Sensible men were not thick on the ground these days and hardly any gentlemen of their acquaintance would willingly support a woman who advocated for truth and equality. The two friends had decided they would rather die as unmarried curmudgeons than live with men who would stifle them.

No, Anna would not let go of this. She would fight to find her friend.

As she reached the marble steps of the Armstrong-Leeds home, a Boston Police Department carriage rolled to a halt in front. Her heart jumped. That meant Pen had not yet found his sister.

An officer alighted. She didn't know him, but he seemed to recognize her, for he addressed her correctly. It was little surprise, since she was famous for her radical politics and her face had graced many a newspaper—not always favorably. The officer gave his name as Adam Graves.

"Are you here at Prince Penforth's request, Mr. Graves?"

He lifted the brass knocker on the enormous mahogany portal and released it.

"Yes, Your Grace."

Antoine, the family's silver-haired butler, showed them inside and Anna immediately asked whether Libby's mother, Christiana, and her sister Mary, were up to receiving visitors.

"They have not yet emerged from their chambers, Your Grace," Antoine replied, eyeing Mr. Graves who was inspecting the scrollwork on the foyer ceiling. Was he admiring it? Anna was unsure.

"Where is Penforth?"

"In his study." He turned to Mr. Graves. "His Royal Highness is expecting you. Please wait here." He turned back to Anna and bowed. "Please follow me, my lady."

She followed him to Pen's study, one of the few parts of the house she'd never seen. Pen sat behind a large oak desk surrounded by piles of paper and unopened missives.

"Duchess Wrexford is here for you, sir," Antoine announced, unnecessarily given Anna was right on his heels. "As is the police officer you requested. He waits in the entry."

Pen rose slowly from his chair and gave the butler a nod of dismissal. He looked like he'd not slept a wink, but was dressed impeccably in gray trousers, a black morning coat, and a matching vest. His hair, however, was in great contrast to the rest of him; disheveled, as though he'd raked his fingers through the dark silken locks too many times.

His mouth was set in a grim line and his dark eyes assessed her from the top of her upswept hair down to the hem of her dress.

Anna felt a shiver run through her, accompanied by the sense of being trapped, with the study's dark setting further pricking her nerves. The deep brown curtains were drawn together so that only a sliver of the already gloomy light filtered into the room.

"This lighting can't be good for your eyes," she jested, to gain some fortitude against his effect on her.

"Good morning to you, too." He moved toward the study door and pushed it mostly shut, leaving it open just a crack, for propriety she guessed. "What are you doing here?"

Anna rolled her eyes. This man's sense of humor traveled the path of non-existence.

"Are you seriously asking me that?" she said, swallowing hard as he came to stand before her. He towered over her.

"Yes."

Resisting the urge to take a retreating step, she

met his gaze. "I am here to help with the investigation."

Pen did not respond at first. He only pierced her soul with his shadowy gaze, and the effects were paralyzing, for Anna found herself unable to move; unable to break the magnetic aura that gripped her. Finally, he spoke. "No."

She blinked, unsure what he'd just said.

"What?"

"I said no. Meaning you will not be involved in any investigation." He inched closer.

Anna took a step back. "If you're trying to intimidate me, it's not working."

A mocking smile tilted one corner of his mouth. "Yes? Then why are you retreating?"

"I am not." She jutted her chin in an attempt at defiance. "In case you haven't noticed, I like my personal space boundaries respected."

"Go home, Anna."

He turned swiftly and strode back to his desk. There was a hitch in his step. His limp was hardly noticeable on most days, but it appeared as though his injured leg was not being kind to him today. She wanted to ask if there was anything she could do to ease his pain but restrained herself. Pen was cynical enough to misinterpret her concern as either pity or mockery, with the latter being more probable.

She placed her hands on her hips. "I am not going anywhere." She held up her hand and silenced him when he began to speak. "And spare me your nonsense about an investigation being no place for a woman, Penforth."

He quirked a sardonic brow. "Then I shall simply carry you, stuff you in a carriage, and have it take you home. And if you try to come back, I will do it all over again."

A small laugh of outrage escaped her throat. "You wouldn't dare."

He stepped forward, his eyes gleaming dangerously. "Oh, I will."

Would he? Pen was not a man to be trifled with. If he said he would do something, likely he *would* do it.

"This is not fair. Libby is my friend." Her voice reflected her exasperation.

"Anna," he said on a sigh. "Mr. Graves is waiting. I do not like to keep people waiting."

"Go see him. I will stay here," she insisted, folding her arms across her chest.

Ostensibly realizing the futility of arguing further with her, Pen left the room. Anna smiled. There was still some hope of convincing him to allow her to help.

She took advantage of her time alone in his study to have a good look at where he spent a substantial part of his day. Darker shades of brown dominated the room, from the wood paneling to the parquet floor. And the olive-green upholstery of the twin wingback chairs facing the dark marble fireplace set just the right tone, declaring the place a man's territory.

Anna fingered the sails of the miniature ship on the desk, wondering if he missed the sea. She rather thought he did.

Moving to the enormous bookcase that occupied most of the wall on the left side of the study, she traced the leather-bound volumes before picking out one with no name on the spine. She was about to open it when the door swung open and Pen walked in.

Anna dropped the book. He gave her a bemused look before picking up a paper from the desk.

"You're still here?"

"I-I was just examining your shelf," she said self-consciously.

"Well, you're not going to find any of my dark secrets there. Come." He waved for her to follow him.

"You have dark secrets?" Her boots clicked

rapidly on the floor as she tried to keep pace with him.

"Everyone has dark secrets, Anna."

She frowned. "I don't."

He glanced askance at her. "Of course not. I don't suppose you do."

Anna blinked in surprise. Was that an attempt at humor?

He led her up the stairs and down the hallway before stopping in front of Christiana's chambers.

She looked up at him, confused. "What are we doing here? I thought you were going to allow me to speak with Mr. Graves."

Pen's hand stilled on the door handle and he turned his impenetrable eyes at her. "Mr. Graves has already left. He has all the information he needs to begin a proper investigation." He paused. "Mother could use your company," he added after a moment.

"Oh, so you've decided on my usefulness, hmm?"

"Must you turn everything into an argument, Anna?"

"Yes. Yes, I must." She folded her arms.

He sighed. "Anna, my mother is rather distraught."

"And you've decided I am the best person to

console her? Libby disappeared in my house, under my watch. I am only going to add to her distress."

"I don't think so."

"I can't do this, Pen. I care about your mother and would love to give her some comfort, but I can't under these circumstances."

"All right," Pen said, running his fingers through his hair. "You may be correct. Come, I'll arrange a carriage to get you home."

Anna closed her eyes, feeling conflicted. This was hard. On one hand, she wanted to be there for Christiana; on the other, she could very well make matters worse. There was only one way to find out.

"No, I'll do it," she said quietly.

He opened the door and Anna tentatively walked in ahead of him. Christiana was in the sitting area adjoining the bedroom, still in her night clothes. She gave Anna a wan smile.

Anna didn't quite know what to say as she sat beside the older woman. She looked to Pen for help but he gave her nothing.

"Christiana...I...I don't know what to say."

"It's all right, Anna. We're all shaken up by this."

"We'll find her, I promise." She gave the older woman's hand a small reassuring squeeze.

"Her reputation is *ruined*." Christiana's mouth twisted in a grimace.

Anna was again lost for words. How did one console a mother whose unwed daughter had possibly been kidnapped?

"Have you spoken to the police?" she asked Pen.

"Yes, Mother, and an investigation has begun. A thorough search of both houses will be carried out."

She waved a dismissive hand. "What good will that do? They should be searching the city."

"They will do that, too. And there may be clues at Wrexford House, or here, that lead us to Libby."

Christiana dabbed at her eyes with an embroidered lace handkerchief and sniffed. "You'll stay a bit longer?" She directed the question to Anna.

Anna's heart twisted in her chest. "Of course, I will." At least there was something she could do right now.

MR. GRAVES RETURNED WITH HIS DEPUTY TO search the house an hour later and Pen refused to allow Anna to even be in the same room as the search party, claiming she might get in the way. The search yielded nothing, just as Anna had suspected it might. If anything were to be found, it would likely be at her own home, where Libby had been staying.

She refused Pen's offer of a carriage, preferring to travel the short distance on foot. He insisted on accompanying her. "You can't keep me from the search in *my* house," she challenged as they walked back to Wrexford House.

"Granted, I can't, but it doesn't change my decision."

If he would not allow her to take part in his investigation, she would start one herself. Whoever found Libby first…

She pulled herself up in her thoughts. It didn't matter who found her friend first. This was not a competition.

When they reached home and entered the guest suite Libby had occupied, everything was as they'd left it the night before. Everything, except the window.

The window was wide open.

CHAPTER FOUR

*P*en heard Anna's sharp intake of breath. "Oh, no."

"What is it?" he asked. "Why is the window open?"

"The staff must have opened it to air the room."

"Good Lord, Anna!" He swore, almost under his breath. "Why would you allow them to do that?"

"I didn't," she returned. "I left instructions before leaving home this morning."

He clenched his jaw so hard he thought his teeth would shatter from the force. This was one of the reasons he'd wanted her to remain here; so that nothing was tampered with.

"I asked you to stay home, Anna."

Her blue eyes flashed with something like anger. "Are you blaming *me* for this, Penforth?"

"Yes."

Someone cleared their throat from down the hall. Pen turned to see Anna's butler Webb leading Mr. Graves and his deputy toward them. He would have to deal with Anna at a later time.

As though she could guess what he was thinking, she brushed past him and the detectives, and disappeared downstairs.

"Shall we, Your Highness?" Mr. Graves asked, pulling a small notebook and a pencil from his coat pocket.

Pen gave him a nod and the police officers entered and looked around. The result was much like that of his own house. Nothing was found to point in any direction whatsoever.

"We've got nothing, sir. No signs of anyone breaking in, no signs of a struggle either." Mr. Graves shrugged. "It looks like the room was left in a hurry. We don't have anything to go on, here. Are you sure the young lady in question didn't simply…"

"I'm sure," Pen said through gritted teeth. "My sister would never disappear like this without explanation."

The policeman nodded. "Quite right, sir. Quite right."

"You need to search the city. I have given you a

portrait for reference. That should be enough for you to start." Pen towered over Graves, deliberately using his height and large frame to intimidate.

The police officer swallowed nervously. "Yes. Yes, of course. We will get started on that immediately, sir."

Pen stood in the room long after they'd left, taking deep even breaths to tamp down his rising choler. He was angry with the police, angry with Anna, but most of all, he was angry with himself. He'd failed in many things, but he did not want to fail in protecting his sister.

Yet, it would appear that he had.

"Webb was the one who opened the window," Anna said softly behind him.

He didn't turn. Neither did he show any indication of hearing her.

"The room was starting to smell from the drenched carpet. He didn't think opening the window would affect the investigation."

Her pause could only mean that she was waiting for him to respond.

When he did not, she said, "Blame me all you want, but leave Webb out of it."

He had no intention of confronting her butler for tampering with the room.

"Did they find anything of note?" she asked.

"No," he finally answered.

"So, what is the next step?"

He turned to face her then, taking slow predatory steps toward her. "The next step for you is to stay out of this."

She jutted her chin out. "You've said as much. Many times. The thing is, no one knows Libby as I do. You're going to need me."

"I don't think so."

He knew he was not being fair, but he didn't know how to behave any other way. Without meeting her gaze or saying anything more, he walked past her and out of the house.

ANNA WAS NO FOOL. IF PENFORTH WANTED TO carry out his investigation alone, that was his problem. But she couldn't sit at home and do nothing.

Tears heated the back of her eyes and she tried, furiously, to blink them away.

She'd failed Libby.

Yes, her friend was a woman grown, but she still needed protection.

Anna lowered herself onto the bed, her heart leaden with loss, guilt, regret, and self-derision. She wished her mother was home. She would know what to do.

What *would* her mother do?

"Sitting here, hating yourself and hating Penforth won't get you anywhere," she would say.

Anna sat up and looked about. She'd been kept out when the room was being searched but she could tell the police had not been thorough because it looked as though nothing had been disturbed. They obviously didn't really believe Libby was taken and must have only conducted a cursory search of the space.

Starting with the drawer by the side of the bed, Anna began to go through every item. She found a stack of letters tied together with a pink velvet ribbon.

Forgive me, Libby, but I have to read these to find you.

After more than an hour of reading, Anna realized most of them seemed to be nothing more than correspondences with distant relatives, friends, and pen friends; giving no clue. She put the letters away and began to look through clothing, dress pockets, the chest at the foot of the bed, and even under the bed. Still nothing.

She was tumbling the pillows when she found a small brown leather book beneath the pile; a journal of some sort. She sat on the bed and began to read, noting nothing of consequence until she reached the last entry which included a date and a location.

Tomorrow's date.

"*Eureka!*" Anna jumped up in triumph.

She had to find the place indicated in the journal, and she had to find it on the morrow.

This was their first real clue, and she hoped it would lead to something tangible. She might even manage to find her friend and bring her home before anyone outside the family realized she'd been gone.

THE FOLLOWING DAY

Pen was going to need Anna's help. It would take a lot to put aside his pride and go to her, but there was no other way. He had spent most of the night stalking the fog-covered streets, speaking to anyone he came across; even looking at posters of crimes on the notice boards in the hopes of finding something that would lead him to Libby. He found nothing.

This incident had made him realize how little he knew his sister. But Anna had been right. She knew her better than anyone.

He tossed back the last of his brandy and set the snifter down, then picked up his greatcoat from the back of the wingback chair by the hearth and his hat from the nearby side table. He moved quietly through the still-dark house. His mother had remained in her room yesterday, and although it was almost seven in the morning, he did not expect she would come out today either. Mary had no inkling of what was happening. She presumed their mother was merely unwell.

When Antoine opened the front door for him, he wondered briefly what the man thought. He was uncertain whether the rest of the servants were aware of his sister's absence, but Antoine knew, and Pen was grateful the butler wasn't one to talk. Gossip traveled faster than trains, and if word got out, the scandal they would be facing could crush their family. Not only would Libby's reputation be ruined, but Mary could kiss goodbye any hopes of a successful debut season. Pen would do everything in his power to secure as much discretion as he could.

The Wrexford butler showed him to the same salon he'd retreated to on the night of the soirée. That night now felt like many moons ago. A portrait of Anna and her parents called out to him and he walked forward to take a closer look. She was much younger, a teen. And while her mother sat primly, focusing on the painter, Anna's attention appeared to be somewhere else; as if she was impatient, ready to take flight and head off on some grand adventure.

He wondered what it was like for her to grow up without any siblings; wondered if she had been lonely and sought Libby to fill the emptiness. He could relate to that loneliness. It had become his constant friend. Where her loneliness was likely a companion dressed in pretty colors and sophistication, his was a dark, cold shadow that had covered him and stayed his mind from letting in even the tiniest finger of light. It had become so much a part of his psyche that its presence had even kept him sane at sea when a storm would sporadically wash in and claim some of his men. It was the secret voice that heartened him to fire the cannon at the enemy ship.

Anna wanted to replace her loneliness with his sister. He was disinclined to let go of his. There was a strange solace in its embrace.

He knew when Anna arrived and lingered at the door before entering. He felt her presence keenly.

When he turned to greet her, he was arrested by a sight he'd not quite been prepared for. The blue of her eyes was as magnetic as the sea and her apparent lack of sleep did not dull the color at all.

They were just eyes, he told himself. But his regard moved from her eyes to the rest of her; while her deep red dress accentuated her artless sensuality, it was her poise that moved him the most.

He could understand why society courted her attention despite her notoriety. Her very presence was commanding. She was magnificent.

"Good morning." He bowed stiffly.

"Good morning, Your Highness," she returned coldly.

Your Highness? What had he been expecting? He'd been a cad the previous day.

She moved to a powder-blue damask chair and lowered her frame into it, her expectant gaze leveling with his.

"Are you going to tell me why you're here or are you going to continue staring?"

Anna appeared to be expecting an apology. *Should* he apologize? He supposed he should if he wanted her cooperation.

"I want to apologize for the way I acted yesterday. It was most unfair of me."

She released a breath and slightly looked away. "You apologize now because you seek my help." She turned back and speared him with a pointed stare. "You would never stoop, otherwise."

It was true.

A small sly smile curved her pretty mouth. "I told you."

"Please, don't gloat."

"I don't see why I shouldn't."

"Anna, I didn't come here to argue. I've not slept in two days—"

"Neither have I—" she began to interrupt and he held up a hand.

"Will you just help me?"

She pursed her lips and allowed the moment to draw out. A part of him knew she would do this, milk her moment of triumph for all it was worth. Finally, she said, "I would rather not."

Jesus Christ!

"You're punishing me, aren't you?" he accused.

An insouciant shrug moved her shoulder. "No, I am not. I simply think you will be rather difficult to work with. I would *rather* not work with you. But I will."

He combed a hand through his hair in aggravation. He was already exhausted, and she was further draining him.

She released a sigh. "I made a discovery last night." She reached into her dress pocket and pulled out a small brown leather book. "There's a date and an address written here."

She showed him, and sure enough, there was an entry made the day before Libby disappeared, but he was lost as to its significance.

"I think Libby was planning to meet someone at this location *today*. I found something else, too." She flipped the pages to the very back of the book before handing it to him.

October 16th, 1891

I don't get flutters and I am most certainly not in possession of the proclivity to succumb to the male charm, but Sir Anthony's letters are beginning to stir feelings inside of me. Perhaps I should respond to see where this could lead us.

Pen looked sharply at Anna after reading. "She was in correspondence with an admirer? That seems…out of character."

Libby did not respond to admirers. If anything, she was positively annoyed by them. He'd long given up trying to marry her off. There was something far greater happening here. He frowned.

"Yes," Anna replied. "I did find a stack of letters last night and went through about half of them, but found nothing from any admirer. If we go back and check the rest, we might find the alluded correspondence."

Pen chuckled darkly. Anna had found the clues when everyone else had missed them. He'd all but underestimated her.

"Lead the way," he said.

A fine eyebrow shot up but she did not say anything. He followed her to Libby's room, the sway of her body undoing his concentrated effort to not be affected by her. The relief that engulfed him when she divided the letters into two and gave him half to go through brought about the realization of how tightly wound he'd been; this was a welcome distraction.

"Here," she announced after what seemed like hours.

Pen looked up at Anna's glittering eyes. She'd found the right letter by the look of it, earning yet another point. Not that this was a competition or anything. He collected the letter and read it.

September 4th, 1891

My dear Lady Elizabeth,

My journey through the West has been most educating, but at the same time, it has awakened a yearning to share such outstanding experiences with a kindred spirit. Someone with equal inclinations to explore the world and see it for its true possibilities.

My dearest, Libby, forgive my directness, but you have set a fire I cannot seem to quench. I want to journey the world with you and advocate by your side if you will have me.

I am returning to Boston soon and although I would love more than anything to call upon you at home, I fear the sort of welcome I may receive from your brother. It would mean the world to me if you could meet me at The Blue Hunter in Cambridge on October 18th.

I shall wait for you there all day.

Yours truly,

Sir Anthony Hart

They found several other letters and read them. Libby and this Sir Anthony Hart had begun their correspondence as pen-friends and advanced beyond that. She was meant to meet him today.

Until they could prove otherwise, he was their prime suspect.

"I need to send a messenger to fetch Mr. Graves now," Pen stated.

CHAPTER FIVE

Mr. Graves arrived at Wrexford House quicker than Anna had anticipated and this time he came alone. Pen had him sit down and read all the letters Sir Anthony had sent Libby. Anna trusted her intuition and it had never failed her; it convinced her now that Sir Anthony was responsible for Libby's disappearance. Pen seemed to believe the same.

After reading those missives, however, Mr. Graves' reaction was not what Anna was expecting. "Sir," he began, "We appear to have an elopement on our hands."

Pen's expression quickly turned stormy. "What?"

"These letters are from a lover and he has asked to meet with her ladyship—"

"Yes, but she disappeared before the set meeting date."

Mr. Graves shook his head. "I am sorry, sir, but this looks very much like an elopement. I am afraid there is nothing more we can do."

Pen took a step toward Mr. Graves and Anna watched as the officer jumped up and retreated, his eyes widening. Anyone would cower if they had a man like Pen advancing on them like that.

"There is nothing you can do?" He spoke slowly, each word an obvious threat.

The officer's eyes darted around the room as though he was looking for an escape route. Unfortunately, Pen had backed him into a wall, flanked by two enormous bookcases.

"I know it is very hard to receive such news, but it is the truth. Your sister has eloped." The officer's voice almost squeaked.

Oh, that was the wrong thing to say, Anna thought as she braced herself for Pen's reaction. Before her next thought had any chance to materialize, Pen had grabbed Mr. Graves by the collar.

"You are useless," he snarled, then dragged him across the room and threw him out the door. "Get out!"

Anna almost felt sorry for the man…almost.

How dare he insinuate an elopement? Her friend would never agree to such a thing. *Never.*

She unclenched her teeth and let out a breath. Since the police did not believe Libby to be abducted, there was only one thing to do.

"I am going to Cambridge to find this person," she said.

"And I am coming with you."

She couldn't argue with him now, and as much as she believed herself to be a brave woman, she had to admit the thought of being accompanied by Pen created a level of comfort and security. Besides, he had a right to be there for his sister.

"My lady." Anna turned her head toward the salon doors to find Webb. He bowed and said, "Miss Harper is here for you."

"Now? What on earth is she doing here?" she asked. "It is early for visitors."

"Shall I tell her you are unavailable? Indisposed, perhaps?" Webb asked.

"That would be goo—"

"We will see her," Penforth interjected, his tone and his eyes deterring any dissent that might have come from Anna.

A confused Webb looked from his employer to the powerful man dominating the room, uncertain whose orders to follow. Anna simplified the choice for him, not out of concession, but out of propriety. She would not be seen arguing with Penforth by the servants. Not even one who had known her since childhood.

She inclined her head toward Webb. "See that she's settled in the drawing room," she instructed calmly, despite the ire rising within. "I'll be with her shortly."

No sooner had the butler departed than she turned her displeasure toward Pen. "You can't come to my house and act like it's yours."

His eyes narrowed. "Miss Harper is your friend, is she not?"

"I wouldn't call her my friend, but we are acquainted."

"Then you know of a certain flaw of hers that often disallows her to keep things to herself."

He had a point. They must not allow Edith to learn anything of what was going on, and to do that, they would have to accommodate this social call.

However, she still found his attempts to take control whenever and however he wanted positively irksome.

Penforth held out his hand. "Shall we?" Anna ignored his hand and after a moment, he rolled his eyes. "After you." He motioned for her to precede him.

They found Edith sitting primly in the drawing room with an expectant smile on her face. The minute she took note of their presence—Penforth's in particular—she rose to her feet with an excited air.

"Your Highness," she began with a simper that only served to make her look ridiculous. "I did not expect to see you here."

"I came to see Anna, Miss Harper."

The guest's face fell instantly and the hand she'd been proffering to him for a kiss hung limply in the air. "You call her by her Christian name?"

"Yes, I have leave to use it."

Edith's fine brows knit together in a frown and her eyes misted. "I have given you leave to use my Christian name, too."

Pen turned to face Anna, a small mysterious smile on his lips and an even more mysterious gleam in his eyes. He was up to something and she did not have a good feeling about it. "I would rather remain on formal terms with ladies I am not courting and ladies who are not relatives of mine."

Edith's mouth fell open. "You're courting Lady Anna?" She looked appalled, as though Anna did not deserve to be courted. It annoyed Anna.

"Yes," Pen said, taking Anna's hand in his.

She wanted to pull her hand out of his grasp and ask him to cease this nonsense, but curiosity was the stronger urge and she let the scene play out.

"You can't court *her*. She..." Her eyes met Anna's and she didn't complete her statement.

"She what?" Pen asked with something like amusement in his voice.

"She is not nice."

"I am not nice?" Anna was surprised by that revelation.

Edith's eyes narrowed. "She believes in…*women's suffrage*." She almost whispered the last part, as if the very speaking of it were an appalling thing.

"You say that as if it's something bad." Pen's matter-of-fact response shocked Anna. She drew in a breath and held it. *Did he mean that?*

"Of course it is!" Edith cried. "Anna, you know how I feel about Prince Armstong-Leeds, yet you allowed him to court you. Friends don't do that."

Anna's free hand went up to massage her temple. What had Pen gotten her into?

"Forgive me, Miss Harper, but I rather think this is not Anna's fault."

Anger flashed in the visitor's eyes. "I will not forgive you for this." Her words were still directed at Anna. Grabbing her purse from the sofa she'd erstwhile occupied, she made for the drawing room exit.

"Was there something you needed?" Anna called after her.

Edith Harper was a woman of routine and calling upon Anna before noon was very uncharacteristic, to say the least.

She paused at the door and turned. Her eyes were cold and unforgiving. "I heard a rumor that Libby is missing so I came to confirm."

Anna's heart sank, and Pen's handhold slackened.

"Libby is fine," Anna said.

"I know of the police search, Anna, so you can quit pretending."

"What are you going to do with this information?" Pen stepped forward, challenging Edith.

"I wanted to offer my help, but now I think I'll just sell the story to *The Brahmin Times*."

"You will do no such thing," Pen countered.

She pursed her lips thoughtfully. "I have a better idea. You could *buy* the story from me."

"You can't mean that, Edith," Anna said, her stomach turning. Edith was not the fool she'd thought. It was a smart move, blackmailing them.

And if it wasn't so wrong, Anna might have complimented her for it.

"Oh, I mean it, Anna. I am sick of playing second fiddle to you. You get all the attention and glory while I get nothing. *Nothing!*" Edith had lost her control now. "Do you know how hard it is to live in your shadow?"

"Listen, this is just a story we came up with to explain the time we're spending together to solve Libby's disappearance. We are not courting."

"Too late, Anna. I don't believe you. And even if it's true, I am not letting this go."

"Miss Harper, please have a seat and let us discuss how we handle this." Pen beckoned for her to sit.

Returning to the sofa and lowering herself onto it, Edith gave Anna a look that said, *I have won.*

"What do you want?" he asked.

She quoted a hefty amount. "That, or marriage. To you."

Pen swore under his breath and ran his hand through his hair. After what appeared to be a moment's contemplation, he said. "I'll pay you."

"Pen, you can't do that," Anna said, taking hold of his arm and pulling him aside. "It's a lot of money."

"And Libby is my sister, with a reputation to

repair." His eyes narrowed. "Don't tell me you think marrying that woman is the better option."

"She likes you."

"More reason to avoid being snared by her. And there will be stipulations. I am not just going to hand money to her without any insurance."

That made Anna feel better, but only slightly.

"Wait here for me to make the appropriate arrangements," he said to Edith before leaving.

Anna stared at Edith. "I understand you have problems with me, but Libby is your friend. Why would you want to hurt her?"

Edith's mouth twisted with disdain. "Oh, you're not the only one I have a problem with. Lady Elizabeth has even less patience with me."

It was true that Libby had less tolerance for Edith's histrionics than Anna, but it was not reason enough for Edith to be this cruel.

"So you'll happily destroy her life?"

She shrugged. "I am not the one who made her disappear, Anna. I simply put myself in a position to take advantage of any opportunity that may arise."

"If word gets out, Libby's reputation will be in tatters. Think about what this will do to her family…to little Mary, who is yet to come out."

"Her brother has gone to take care of it, has he

not?" She smiled. "You know, at this point, I am not as keen on gaining Sir Penforth's favor for courtship as I had earlier been. I am going to walk out of this house today a very wealthy woman. That surely surpasses my desire of marrying him. After all, his wealth was his main attraction."

Anna could no longer listen to Edith talk. She rang for the butler and stalked out of the room when Webb arrived.

"Watch her. Don't let her out of your sight," she instructed. "And let me know when Penforth returns."

"Of course, Your Grace."

CHAPTER SIX

*P*en was unsettled by Miss Harper's blackmail, but he was not foolish enough to just hand over that kind of money without protective measures in place. Miss Harper was something of a prattler. She could easily take his money and still sell the story.

Paying her off would buy some time to concoct a reasonable explanation for Libby's absence, so that even if the woman did talk, in the end it would not matter.

He also knew something that Anna did not. The Harpers' finances were in dire straits. Word in the clubs was that Miss Harper's brother Johnathan had more gambling debt than he could ever repay. It came as no surprise that she would try to capitalize on his sister's plight.

As his eyes moved over the contract his attorney had drawn up on short notice, he couldn't help but wonder how Anna felt about all of this. She was angry, of that he was certain. This was his fault. If he had not told Edith that lie about himself and Anna, the stupid woman would not have snapped and decided to blackmail them.

He would fix this. He had no choice.

"It will suffice," he said to his attorney, James Wrotham.

"Excellent. All that's needed now is her signature. She will only be able to access the funds after her ladyship has been found and after her discretion has been verified. Beyond that time, of course, we can't necessarily stop her talking."

Pen nodded and rose from his chair, pulling a watch from his vest pocket to check the time. It was twelve past one in the afternoon. If things had not taken an ugly turn this morning he and Anna would have been at the Cambridge location looking for Sir Anthony by now. Nevertheless, they could still make it before the day's end.

Miss Harper had made herself very comfortable in the Wrexford House drawing room with tea and cakes. The sight of food reminded Pen that he'd not eaten anything today. *Later*. He would deal with food later.

"Let's get to business," he said to Miss Harper. She dropped her teacup back onto the saucer with a loud clatter. He waited for her to compose herself before nodding at his lawyer, who handed her the agreement.

She perused the contents and when she was finished, looked up at him with a frown. "This isn't fair."

"Don't talk to me about fairness, Miss Harper." He held out a ball pen. "Sign it."

With deliberate slowness, she scrawled her signature. When she gave him back the contract, the smugness was gone from her expression. That change assured him of the rightness of his action.

Anna was standing to one side, watching them all. "Now," she announced in an icy tone. "Get out of my house and don't ever come back, *Miss* Harper."

Pen turned to look at Anna. She was holding herself stiffly, and not hiding her displeasure. He handed the signed agreement to Wrotham, who departed immediately.

Anna immediately attacked. "Are you happy?" she seethed.

"No, I am not. But it's settled now."

"This could have been avoided, Penforth, and you know it."

"I was in your house before breakfast, and you had not received me in any of your drawing rooms. Don't you think that would have drawn some suspicion? Saying I am courting you was the best excuse I could come up with to protect your reputation."

"Fine." She exhaled audibly. "Not that I have a great reputation to uphold. *You* know. *Suffrage*."

For a moment they shared a quick smile, and then he saw her shoulders slump slightly. "You just parted with almost a quarter of your fortune," she said.

What he had potentially given Edith was not even one-tenth of his fortune, but he didn't correct her. Not even his family knew the extend of his actual wealth. He'd invested in steel manufacture as soon as he'd left the Navy following his injury. The decision had proven a profitable one for Pen himself, and for the family as a whole.

"Miss Harper is not going to get those funds easily. I've made sure of that."

"Penforth," she drew out his name, "you can't be controlling my life like this. If my father had not thought me worthy of inheriting his title, then a male cousin I've never met would be standing here now. My mother trusted me enough to leave this house in my care and depart for England indefinitely. Now I need you to afford me the same respect. I need you to let me have a say in how we manage things." Her voice was low and soft, but the message in her words was clear.

She wanted him to regard her as his equal. *Impossible.*

"Until Libby is found, I will remain in control and that's final."

Anna opened her mouth as though to say something but then clamped it shut. He didn't like disagreeing with her, but someone would have to make her understand that the equality utopia she was dreaming of was beyond reach.

"A lot of time has been wasted, but I can still make it to Cambridge. Though now I have decided. I am going alone."

Her head snapped up and her eyes flared, predictably. "And you expect me to remain here." She made a dramatic gesture. "Prepare both houses for Libby's return, right?"

"I think that's a splendid idea."

"You are mad." She stood up. Her fire was rather remarkable, really. "Who discovered the location in the first place?"

She had a point but he did not indulge her with a response.

"I am not going to waste any more time

arguing," she announced. "Do whatever you want, Penforth. I don't care."

He became suspicious of her concession. Even more so when she brushed past him to leave. His hand shot out to take hold of her arm.

"Where are you going?"

"To find my best friend, of course."

Never in his thirty-two years had he had to deal with a woman as stubborn as Anna. "Fine," he grated. "We go together."

"Come on then." Anna already had a carriage waiting in front of Wrexford House.

Of course she did. Pen ground his teeth again, wondering if they would remain intact beyond the next few hours.

She jumped up into the carriage without needing help. As he climbed up behind her, an unfamiliar feeling washed over him. A feeling akin to tenderness. He almost laughed at the ridiculousness of it.

She was a beautiful woman, there was no doubt about that, but he had seen his fair share of beautiful women and been unmoved by them. So, what was different about this particular beautiful woman?

Everything, his brain yelled.

"Penforth?" Her fine brows drew together when he paused in the doorway.

He shook his head and sat opposite her on the rear-facing seat, avoiding her eyes.

Anna gave the roof of the carriage a knock and they started moving. Pen seldom felt uncomfortable, but the direction his thoughts had taken and Anna's voice breaking into those thoughts had him feeling invaded.

"Hmm?" He thought he heard her say something.

"You've not heard a single word, have you?"

"Forgive me. I am a bit distracted."

"I can see that," she said wryly. "You've been staring at this pillow beside me for ages."

Had he? His eyes focused on the velvet pillow.

"I asked if we have a plan for when we get there."

"Simultaneously search for Libby and Sir Anthony. We don't know what he looks like, but we have the location, and Libby's portrait to show around. If luck favors us, we should uncover something."

A grimace twisted her mouth. "I don't believe in luck," she muttered.

"That's an unusual thing for a woman to say."

He shifted his focus to her face, trying to read her expression. He got nothing.

"Really?" Her tone turned acerbic. "Why do you say that?"

"Women usually believe in luck." He paused, contemplating the wisdom of saying the last words, and then added, "And fairytales." Instantly, he regretted it.

A disdainful laugh escaped her and her cerulean-blue eyes darkened. "I'll bet you think it a weakness; to believe in luck *and* fairytales."

She seemed ready to defend those of her gender who did believe in those things, regardless of how she felt herself. Her spirit was admirable, and Pen wondered how she contained all that fire within.

He swiftly held up a placating hand. "Before you send me to the butcher, I'll have you know that I find it fascinating. Now, I don't believe in fairytales myself, but I am a strong believer in luck."

"*You?*" Her brows shot up in disbelief. "*You* believe in luck?"

"Is that hard to fathom?"

"Penforth, you have the disposition of a cynic."

He chuckled. "I *am* a cynic, and a skeptic, too." He watched the play of emotion on her face; surprise, curiosity… admiration?

Maybe he was seeing things.

Or feeling things, his inner voice suggested. He trampled it as quickly as it registered. There was no room for such sentiment. There never had been and there never would be.

"You can't be all those things and still believe in luck. It doesn't work like that," she said.

He shrugged. "It does for me. I would not be walking if fate had not looked kindly upon me."

Anna lowered her eyes. "I see."

She was not going to challenge him anymore, he was certain.

"How did it happen?"

He didn't pretend to misunderstand what she meant by *it*. He had succeeded in temporarily dispelling her challenging spirit but awakened her curiosity in its place. Should he share tales of his wounds? Women loved to hear about how men got injured while protecting them or their country.

But he'd been defending no one except himself when the bullet pierced his knee and almost rendered the entire limb obsolete. A drunk officer had lost a game of cards to him and they had brawled it out. Dissatisfied with the outcome of the brawl, the officer had pulled out his pistol.

"I was shot," he said peremptorily.

Heedless of his dismissing tone, she pressed him

for more information. "How did you get shot? Was it in the line of duty?"

"Good Lord, Anna! Why do you want to know?"

"I have known your family for over a decade but I know nothing about *you*."

"And that is the first thing you ask?"

"It's an important part of who you are."

Why was she interested in knowing him now? The few times he'd been home for holidays during his naval career, Anna and Libby had been too busy perusing the newspapers and dreaming of leading the women's revolution. And when he'd returned for good after his injury, she had avoided him altogether.

"You never cared before." That sounded petty, he knew.

She folded her arms across her middle. "Really, Penforth? You close yourself up and push everyone away, yet think they don't care about you."

Perhaps she was right. Had he pushed everyone away? Perhaps she actually did care. And perhaps not.

"You were so bitter when you came back," she said.

"Do you blame me? I thought I would never

walk again. Every physician I saw gave me the same low odds."

"But you beat them. Your limp is hardly noticeable, but your manner remains the same."

"I suppose I *like* being this way." He knew his darkness already. It was easier to deal with than any alternative.

"Then you're never going to have many friends."

He laughed. "You think I care about friendship?"

Anna stared at him in disbelief. "Aren't you afraid of dying alone?"

"Loneliness is an old and familiar companion, Anna."

"I pity you," she said, and her low sad voice vexed him.

"What are you going to do about it?" he mocked. "You are a problem-solver. Tell me how to solve my problem."

"Don't patronize me, Penforth."

He was beginning to like it when her eyes flared. The flash of spirit both amused and beguiled him.

He bowed his head. "My apologies, Your Grace." There! That should further rile her.

The small velvet pillow flew through the

confined carriage space and collided with his face. He fell back in his seat, laughing.

He, Penforth Armstrong-Leeds, was laughing. When was the last time he'd laughed? The recollection of such an event was beyond him. He tossed the pillow back at her, making sure he did not throw it with too much force; and two pillows came back to him…with some force.

"You were being gentle," she accused, laughing with him.

"I am a gentleman."

Their eyes held for a long moment, and her face softened as her pert lips curved up into an alluring smile. That feeling he'd erstwhile dismissed returned, challenging him to unmask it, reveal its truth.

"So tell me, why don't you believe in luck?" Pen asked more to squelch that bothersome feeling than to sate his curiosity.

"I grew up alone and during that time, all I ever wanted was a sister or brother to share my adventures with. My mother had gotten with child four times and lost them all. The fifth time, it took, and we all got very excited. She gave birth to a boy." Her thick lashes came down to conceal the pain he saw briefly in the depth of her eyes. "He died after three months. My father had no male successor, at least not a direct one. His title and everything entailed was meant to pass to a male cousin. After my dear brother's death, Father applied for permission to pass the title to me. Luck has had very little play in my family's life, Pen."

"I am sorry, Anna," he said solemnly.

"Perhaps it is not healthy, but I hold onto Libby to somehow fill the void of being alone." She laughed a little. "I could marry, but I'd rather not if that is my sole motivation to seek a partner."

In some ways, he and Anna were not very different. Though she was not afraid to let the people she cared about know how she felt and that made her more courageous than him. He respected her for that.

"You are not altogether intolerable," he said.

"Is that supposed to be a compliment?"

He smiled. "I think it is."

"You are in dire—"

The carriage jolted and Anna lurched forward.

$\mathcal{A}$nna's breath stuck in her throat when she was thrown from her seat. Pen threw out his arms to catch her, but she landed on top of him.

"We must have hit a rut in the road," he said.

Their closeness was dizzying and he looked quite comfortable, as if he was used to being in such situations.

"You can let me go now," she croaked.

He grinned the grin of a libertine and lightly stroked her cheek with a finger. The feather-light touch sent a wave of sensation through her body, dulling her senses to everything else.

"I am not holding you," he murmured, his voice deep and decadent.

When he brushed her hair from her face, she

knew she had to get away. She didn't trust her own mind with him this close.

Think, Anna.

The carriage gave another jolt and this time, his arms did encircle her—around her waist, to be precise—and she stopped breathing altogether. She watched, entranced, as his face drew closer and his dark eyes softened. It was as if she could feel his thoughts, his intentions; they were almost palpable.

Anna wanted to give in to him, she really did, but Penforth was not a man to be trifled with. She would find herself in pieces if they went down this path. Summoning some much-needed willpower from deep within herself, she pulled out of his embrace and pushed herself off him.

"Forgive me," he said quietly after a moment.

She nodded.

The remainder of the journey was made in silence. It would have been more bearable if they had never had that moment. Tension thickened the carriage space and Anna felt like she was sitting on pins. Every now and then, she'd steal a glance up at him but would only be greeted by his profile, for he continued to stare out the window.

He didn't seem happy about what had happened, which made her feel worse. One did not regret something unless they perceived it to be bad.

Her own reaction to him in the past had always unsettled her, but she had never actively disliked feeling this way, until now. The brief tenderness in his gaze and the softness of his touch meant nothing if he ended up regretting his actions.

Lately, despite her aggravation at his condescension, she had found herself yearning to know more about him; to get closer to him. But clearly, Pen didn't reciprocate.

"We're here," he said suddenly, interrupting her thoughts.

Anna stared out the window. They were approaching what appeared to be a stage station, a crossroads connecting different parts of Massachusetts. She already had a bad feeling about Sir Anthony, but seeing the place he'd asked Libby to meet elevated Anna's consternation.

"What manner of man asks a gently-bred lady to meet him in a place like this?"

"One with nefarious intentions," Pen replied grimly, a vein working in his temple.

When the carriage stopped, he turned to her, his demeanor grave. She knew what he was going to say before he said it, and she was tempted to put a finger up to his lips and stop the words.

"You must—"

"Don't even think about it," she said. "I will not agree."

"You didn't hear me out," he complained.

"I don't need to."

"I do the things I do for your safety, Anna."

"Well, I appreciate your concern. But don't you think I will be safer with you than alone here?"

"The coachman and footman will remain here with you. I'll give them a pistol for protection."

"You are a bully."

His jaw dropped.

Without waiting for him—or his approval—she flung open the door and stepped down from the carriage. Glancing up briefly at the overcast sky she realized rain was coming, but that hadn't stopped the bustle of activity at the crossroads. Stagecoaches carried passengers and mail, as well as private and hired carriages that all conveyed people to their respective destinations. Stage stations took in weary travelers, and teams of exhausted horses were exchanged for fresh ones. It was quite a remarkable sight, and Anna felt her spirits lift. One or more of these people could surely give them their next clue.

"I am a bully?" Pen asked, alighting from the carriage.

Anna rolled her eyes. "Why are you surprised?"

"I don't recall making you do something you didn't want to do."

Anna chuckled wryly. "You have been managing my life since that dreadful soirée. If that is not bullying, I don't know what is."

"I apologize," he said.

Her mouth dropped open and then closed. He'd ended the argument with a simple apology.

During the lull in their conversation, he took her hand and tucked it in the crook of his elbow. "Come."

The *Blue Hunter*, the place mentioned in Sir Anthony's missive, was the grandest of all the structures at the crossroads. The inn occupied a central position, with those people scurrying in and out of the Tudor-style building looking similar to Anna and Pen. Was this where the *crème de la crème* of society rested, on their travels? She pulled the edge of her toque down over her face, bending the feather to try to form a disguise.

"That flimsy plume cannot hide your face. You are a popular woman, easily recognizable." Pen, whose eyes were almost completely concealed by his low-sitting derby, remarked.

Why does women's fashion have to be so complicated? Why could I not wear a hat such as his?

Arm in arm and with Anna's head down, they

entered the *Blue Hunter* and went straight for a pale, gaunt man behind the counter. Anna thought he looked like a figure one might find in a Mary Shelley book; stooped and skeletal, with greasy hair and sunken eyes. He straightened his black coat that hung loose on his bony shoulders and turned bleary eyes at them, blinking slowly.

"Welcome to the *Blue Hunter*," he drawled. "The finest establishment at the Cambridge crossroads."

Anna wondered how many times he'd had to repeat that phrase today.

"We're not looking for accommodation. We're looking for someone. May we speak with you privately?" Pen got straight to the point.

"Of course, Sir." The man bowed his head. "Please come with me."

They followed him down a dimly lit hallway to an elaborately furnished salon that smelled faintly of tobacco. This place, too, was dimly lit.

"Would you like to be seated?" he offered.

"No, thank you. We will not stay long." Pen retrieved Libby's portrait from his coat pocket and showed it to him. "Have you seen this woman?"

The man's slender fingers closed over the picture, and he raised it to the single ray of light filtering in through the window to examine it. He took his time studying the picture before giving it back to Pen.

Anna's intuition told her the man knew something. Why else would he take that much time examining the picture?

"No," he said, very slowly. "I am afraid I have never seen her."

The breath she'd been holding in anticipation gushed out in frustration.

"Have you received a guest named Sir Anthony Hart?" Pen asked.

He shook his head. "No."

"May we speak to your colleagues?"

"Employees," he corrected. "I am the sole proprietor of this establishment." Anna was unable to tell if he was affronted by their assumption of him being an employee or not. His tone was as flat as could be.

"Right."

"No one comes in or goes out without my knowledge. There has been no Sir Anthony Hart here."

"Well, then, thank you for your time."

"And good luck in your search," he said, almost pleasantly.

When they exited the inn, Anna huffed out an exasperated breath. "Where to now?"

Pen did not reply immediately. His eyes raked the scene as he seemingly considered what next.

"That innkeeper seemed to know more than he was letting on," she prompted, eventually.

Pen nodded. Finally, he said, "Let's check that place." He pointed with his chin toward a white building with green shutters and purple and yellow flowers in planters hanging on the windows.

It was one of the buildings flanking the *Blue Hunter* with a sign above the entrance that read, *Two Billed Duck*. While the former was more likely the place a man of Sir Anthony's rank would stay, this one obviously catered to the lower classes. Even so, Anna, realized, it should not be entirely ruled out.

A memory constricted her throat and she swallowed against it, taking a deep breath to calm herself.

Pen tugged her close. "Are you all right?"

"I just remembered one of Libby's and my antics."

They had been in England two years prior, visiting Anna's relatives, and had been traveling through London. One of the inns they'd stopped at was called the *Swan With Two Necks*. Anna and Libby had imagined an actual swan with two necks, triggering a laughing spree that had lasted the whole night. They'd laughed at everything and nothing when they should have been sleeping. And the sherry they'd had at dinner only fueled their folly. This had seen them nap throughout the next day's journey.

If Libby saw the *Two Billed Duck* now, she'd no doubt burst out laughing, saying, "Who names these places?"

A shiver ran through her, from the roots of her hair down to the tip of her shod toes.

Pen squeezed her gloved fingers. "We'll find her, Anna."

They had to. She couldn't bear any other outcome.

The *Two Billed Duck* was a busy place with people milling about, and though everyone went about their own business, Anna could feel curious eyes on them when they entered.

A man behind the counter beamed at them as they approached. His eyes did a slow assessment, causing him to beam wider.

"Welcome to the *Two Billed Duck*. How may I be of service?" Not giving Pen or Anna any chance to speak, he continued. "Our establishment boasts the finest chambers, made for our best guests." His smile grew wider. "Guests like yourselves. And of all the stage stations here, we provide the finest dining experience. May I interes—"

"We're here for none of that," Pen cut him off. "We need to speak with you privately."

The man swallowed as his eyes darted from the commanding man towering over him to Anna.

He leaned forward and asked in a whisper, "May I ask what this is about?"

Anna heard Pen growl out an expletive. He was obviously losing patience.

The innkeeper swallowed again and lifted the counter flap for them to pass. "This way, please."

He led them into a back room that looked like an office.

"We are looking for someone." Pen got straight to the point once again, showing him a portrait of Libby. "Have you seen her?"

The man stared at the portrait for a long time and Anna clutched Pen's arm in anticipation.

"I haven't seen her, sorry." He gave Pen back the portrait.

Anna didn't want to be disheartened. There were still two more stage station inns to check.

"Let's go," Pen said, steering her toward the exit.

An idea illuminated her mind. "Wait." She turned to the landlord. "Have you by any chance heard of a Sir Anthony Hart?"

Recognition flared in his eyes and Anna held her breath. He knew something.

"A man bearing that name spent a night here four days ago. He left at noon the following day saying he would return."

"And has he? Returned, that is?"

He shook his head. "He has not."

"What does he look like?" Pen asked.

"He has light-colored hair, similar to yours, my lady. He had gray eyes. And a scar on his temple, right across his brow. Good-looking chap."

"Any other details?" Anna asked.

"He was finely dressed. Not as good as *you*."

It was not a lot of information, hardly enough for them to track him down, but it was information, nevertheless.

Anna fished out some coins from the purse in her pocket and pressed them into his hands. "Thank you, Mr..."

"Abernathy. Ronald Abernathy." he supplied.

"Thank you, Mr. Abernathy."

He beamed beatifically, as though he'd just been promised heaven.

"You gave him money," Pen remarked when they stepped out of the *Two Billed Duck*.

"Is that a bad thing?"

"On the contrary. That was nice of you."

She smiled. "I think he valued the appreciation more than the actual coin."

He paused and turned to look at her. There was that tender look again. "You're very intuitive, Anna."

She could feel the heat his words evoked rising from her neck up to her cheeks.

"Thank you," she murmured, turning her face away from him.

The next stage station—*The Explorer*—looked much like the *Two Billed Duck*, but was busier on the inside. Getting the attention of the landlord took some time. They did not elicit any information from him. The last stage station—the *Blue Blocks*— yielded the same result as the previous one.

Dejection weighed heavily on Anna's shoulders by the time they left the *Blue Blocks*. She'd thought Sir Anthony's description and Libby's portrait would get them somewhere, but it didn't. They were back to where they had started and it was late afternoon already.

"What now?" she asked Pen.

He looked about determinedly. "We ask the carriage drivers."

Anna let out a breath and nodded. There were many carriages and many drivers. "Shall we begin?"

The first driver was hard of hearing, making communication difficult.

"I've never seen her," he shouted. "What did you say the man looked like?"

Anna stared about nervously. Keeping this matter under wraps was important, not just to save Libby's reputation, but for their ultimate success in finding her. Her captors could be anywhere, and they could be alerted of the search which might make them change their course, and subsequently render Anna and Pen's progress useless.

In what could only be deemed an asinine performance, Anna described what Sir Anthony looked like, pointing at the gray sky to indicate the color of his eyes and her light-colored hair to confirm the color of his, then pointing at a horse's tail to describe a queue. The driver stared at her as though she had lost her mind. Only after he'd received a dramatic description of his scar did the driver show any hint of comprehension.

"Oh, I drove him," he said, spreading his lips into a grin that revealed a missing front tooth.

Anna felt hope begin to blossom.

"Where did you drive him to?" she asked quickly. He did not understand her, so she had to yet again demonstrate.

"I dropped him at that stage station four days ago. Didn't see him again."

The growing hope recoiled and shriveled.

"He doesn't have anything new, Pen." Anna choked on a sob.

He took both her hands in his and gave them a reassuring squeeze. "I know, but we have to continue. If he has passed through here, something about him is bound to turn up. There's a chance that Libby did not come here. Let's make finding Sir Anthony our priority." He tucked a finger under her chin and tilted her face up. "It's going to be all right, Anna. I am here."

I am here. She needed that, his presence, his support...his attention, too.

Anna yearned for his attention, and she didn't know what to do to stop that feeling. Denial had led her nowhere and acknowledgment had only caused aggravation.

They'd just turned to locate the next driver when they heard a beckoning hiss from the nearby alley. They ignored it and carried on, until suddenly, something grabbed Anna's sleeve. In a motion so quick it was almost a blur, Pen pushed Anna away and placed himself between her and the supposed attacker.

It was a woman, small in stature and dressed like a woman of the night. Her face was stunning despite the garishness of her cosmetics, with kohl-rimmed eyes, a powder that gave her a sallow pallor, and the rouge that had been drawn over the boundaries of her thin lips beginning to smear. She was quite a sight.

But she didn't frighten Anna.

"What do you want?" Pen asked coolly, shielding Anna with his large powerful frame.

"I heard you talking to Deaf Billy over there," she slurred. "I think I can help."

"What do you know?"

She looked around conspiratorially before leaning forward and whispering, "Follow me."

Pen turned to Anna. "What do you think?"

"She might have some valuable information."

He took hold of Anna's hand and they followed the woman into the alley.

Once they were out of view, she held her hand out. "Pay first."

"What?" Anna was surprised. Pen, however, was not moved by her request. "You said you wanted to help."

"Not freely, Mister." She eyed Pen. "If you don't have money, we could come to some other arrangement." A coquettish smile tipped the corners of her mouth up as she batted her lashes at him. "What do you say, my lord?" She ran a finger with a long red-tinted nail down the lapel of his coat.

Anna wanted to slap her hand away. *How dare she?*

"You will do well to remove your hand from my person," Pen warned, his voice cold and menacing.

She quickly drew her hand away as if burned.

"I am not telling until you pay."

He placed three silver coins in her hand. "Now talk."

"I saw a man that looks like the one you described to Deaf Billy. He was here with a woman yesterday."

"What did the woman look like?" Anna asked, trying not to get hopeful.

"She's pretty." The woman shrugged and made a face. "Dark hair. Dressed nicely like you."

"Is this her?" Pen showed her Libby's portrait.

"I didn't look very well but she looks like that. Yes, I think it is her."

"Did you see where they went?"

She held out her hand, palm open, the greedy wench.

"You're going to have to pay for that, sir."

Grudgingly, Pen placed another three coins in her hand. The woman knew how to make money, Anna would give her that.

"You'd want to ask Arthur Pelham about this because they got into his carriage." She paused as if in thought. "And the woman was drunk. I think she was drunk."

Anna found that odd because Libby never got drunk, at least not to the point where it was obvious to people that she'd imbibed too much.

"Where do we find Arthur Pelham, then?" she pushed.

The woman waved her hand in the direction of the cluster of carriages. "He should be out there somewhere."

Anna looked up at Pen just as he looked down at her. The shared moment felt good. "We have something," she whispered and he smiled.

"It was nice doing business, my lord!" The woman called after them as they exited the alley.

Anna groaned, disgusted by the attention and wanton looks the woman had been giving Pen. It was rather relieving to know that he did not give such women his attention.

Looking down at her hand in his, she smiled inside. In jumping to her rescue—even though it was not required—Penforth had given her a glimpse of himself that he kept concealed from the world; the part of him he would never admit existed —not even to himself. The part that cared.

The sun was going down and fog was stealing in with the dusk, making the hairs on the back of

Anna's neck stand on end. Time was passing and Libby was yet to be found.

They approached a group of drivers clustered together, and every one of them straightened in readiness, no doubt assuming they wanted to be conveyed somewhere.

"We're looking for Arthur Pelham," Pen said.

"He just left. Took some passengers up north," one of the drivers responded.

"Where north?"

He shrugged and shook his head. "I don't know."

"I think I heard him say Lexington," another driver said.

"Lexington is not too far," Anna said to Pen. "We could be there in three hours."

Pen shook his head. "We're not going there."

CHAPTER EIGHT

"Why not?" Anna asked.

"We are not sure we will find him there." Pen explained. "He will be back."

Anna looked exhausted and not just physically. He couldn't drag her all the way to Lexington to hunt down a man who probably didn't have the information they needed. Pelham would return to the crossroads and they would be here to question him when he did.

"Can I have a minute?" Pen said to the driver who had told them of Pelham's supposed whereabouts. A short, skinny man. Skittish, too, from the look of him.

They stepped to the side, out of the others' earshot.

"What's your name?" Pen asked him.

"Clayton," he replied.

"Here's what we're going to do, Clayton. I want to hire you to watch for Pelham."

Clayton instantly became nervous and looked from Pen to Anna and back. "Is he wanted for a crime?"

"No. We want some information from him, that's all."

Visibly relieved, Clayton sighed. "Pelham is my friend. I should hate to see him in trouble."

Pen decided to use the men's friendship to his advantage. He placed his hand on the man's shoulder.

"But he might be in trouble if we don't find him. We need your help, and *he* needs your help."

Clayton took a deep determined breath. "What do I do?"

"When does he return?"

"Oh, likely in the early hours of the morning."

"Good. When he returns, tell him not to go anywhere. We will be back tomorrow morning. Say, eight o'clock."

Pen gave him a handful of silver dollars. "There will be plenty more tomorrow," he said, looking gravely into the man's eyes to show him his sincerity while silently warning him of the consequences should he trifle with them. "Pelham will get a reward too if he complies."

"Of course, sir," Clayton replied with alacrity. "He will be here tomorrow. We both will be here."

Pen smiled. Who didn't want to make quick money? He'd put in place a measure that would ensure they met Pelham when they returned tomorrow. And if that prostitute had indeed told them the truth, then they would know where Sir Anthony had taken Libby.

Anna was smirking when his eyes found her. "What?" he asked.

"I am quite impressed."

"And here I thought I'd be reprimanded by you."

"I'll admit it's not something I would have done, but I nevertheless appreciate your tactful employment of deception and bribery."

"Well, I am no noble soul." He offered her his arm.

"Are we going home now?" She took his arm and they began to walk toward their waiting carriage.

"Yes."

"We've made some progress today, haven't we?"

He looked down at her and was struck by the play of light and shadow on her face. The light

from the street gas lamps made her eyes sparkle and highlighted her soft mouth, while the shadow contoured her face and neck in an artlessly bewitching way.

"Yes, we have." He could remain here, staring at her all night, but he had to get her home safely. "I rather liked that quaint performance you put on for Deaf Billy."

She poked his shoulder playfully. "At least I made an effort to make him understand. What did you do?"

"I made sure Pelham will be here to meet us in the morning. And I paid that woman who told us about Pelham."

"I paid the landlord," she defended.

"Is this a competition, Anna?" They stopped in front of the Wrexford carriage and the driver readied the reins.

"It is when you keep challenging me," she replied with great feeling.

He raised his brows. "Pray, tell me, how I've been challenging you."

"You think I am not capable because I am a woman."

"I—"

"I am good at solving problems!" She cut him off. "You said so yourself. And even though you were being ironic, I know there is some truth to it."

He sighed. Anna exhausted him. "Are you done speaking?"

"Yes." She jutted her chin out and her eyes flashed like they always did when she was riled.

"I do know how capable you are and you did remarkably well today," he conceded in as soft a tone as he could muster. "There is no basis for you to compare yourself to me."

"You're saying we cannot be equals, then?"

Good Lord!

"Anna, I am not saying that." He half laughed and half scolded. "I am not going to let you rope me into that debate." He wagged a finger at her. "No."

She was annoyed, the set of her mouth and that fire swirling in her eyes said as much.

Pen handed her into the carriage and instead of sitting where he'd sat before, he settled beside her in the front-facing seat. The urge to dismiss his desire to be near her was matched and subsequently vanquished by the urge to sate that desire.

Anna made him feel, and he could no longer deny it.

Beside him, he felt her shift slightly and sigh, reminding him of his own weariness—he'd not slept in days—and hunger. As if to echo his thoughts, his stomach growled.

She smiled—he sensed it more than saw it in the darkness. "It's nice to know I am not the only one starving," she murmured.

"All that's keeping me is a few fingers of whiskey."

She chuckled. "At least I had a scone and a cup of chocolate."

His stomach gave a protesting rumble at the mention of scones and chocolate. He glanced out the window at the passing scenery, mentally counting the time until they reached home.

"I hope she's all right," came Anna's whisper. He could feel her disquietude because it mirrored his.

For the first time, he regretted the time he'd not spent with his sister. The time he'd spent brooding and wallowing in anger instead of loving his family. This event had shown him how little he knew of Libby. And Mary? Mary was all but a stranger to him. The realization hit him hard in the solar plexus.

"So do I," he replied, deeply ashamed.

No wonder Anna thought him cold and unfeeling, a man with no regard for people's sensibilities. He had pushed everyone away after his retirement from the Navy.

Despite the choice to end his naval career being entirely in his own hands, its premature end had taken a toll on him; knowing he would never stand on the deck of a ship with his men ready to make the seas safe had been unmanning.

He'd not been officially dismissed. After his injury, he'd come home to convalesce, and just when he'd beaten the odds and regained the mobility of his leg, fate had dealt him a blow. His father died, forcing him to take up the reins as head of the family.

And so far, it seemed, he'd not done a good job of that.

"You are very quiet. What's on your mind?" Anna asked softly.

"I am always quiet," he replied, unsure what to tell her.

"This quiet feels like you're deep in thought."

"How would you know that?"

"I can see it on your face," she said. "Despite the lack of daylight."

"Have you been staring at me?" He turned to look at her.

"Mhmm." She nodded.

"In the darkness."

"It's not entirely dark. There's a little light from the carriage lamps streaming in."

"And did you see anything you like?" *Yes, this should keep her from prying his mind.*

He couldn't see her face well enough to determine the color, but he could tell she was embarrassed by the way she sucked in her lips.

"I was not looking *that* hard."

He chuckled wryly. "Of course you weren't. You were only staring."

"I-I meant...I wasn't looking for anything to like." She turned her face to the window, away from his view.

"You don't have to tell me what you're thinking, but say something...anything," she said after some time had passed. "I don't like the quiet. It makes me think of things."

"The curse of the wandering mind," he murmured.

"Yes. Tell me something about yourself."

Pen took a moment to reply. He had to filter his thoughts first.

"Whenever we visited our relatives in Eskoania when I was a boy, my cousins and I would play pirates. I was a pirate named Captain Striker, feared by merchants and disliked by my fellow pirates."

Anna laughed. "Let me hazard a guess, you looted both parties."

"Yes." His mouth curved up into a smile.

"How did you end up becoming a naval officer then?"

"I grew up and realized what a fantasy it was. The stories make pirates heroic, inciting young boys like myself to tie handkerchiefs on their heads and carry around wooden swords. The sea called me, but I couldn't answer that call as a pirate."

"That's quite noble of you."

"No, it had more to do with the possibility of my father disowning me if I did. I'm not directly in line for the throne—there's a lot of other family members ahead of me in the queue—but a pirate? Oh, that *would* be a disgrace to everyone."

"How was it? The sea."

A sliver of bitterness curled in his chest, constricting the small space. "It gives you a sense of freedom, like you can do anything, go anywhere." He managed a wan smile, hoping it would conceal what he was truly feeling.

"I think I understand. That feeling of standing on the deck of a ship with the wind in your hair and the song of the sea in your heart. The stormy nights that awaken you to your mortality."

"You make it sound romantic. Yes, there is nothing quite like it."

She smiled up at him. "I suppose I *am* a romantic. I love sea travel."

"Imagine doing it perpetually."

"The change must have been very hard for you," she said gently. He could feel her commiseration and although he appreciated the empathy somewhat, he was disinclined to accept it.

Doing so would be akin to exposing weakness.

He had shared quite a bit with her already and was not in possession of enough generosity to share more.

Silence enshrouded them and as Anna turned again to stare out the window, ostensibly becoming engulfed in her thoughts, Pen allowed himself to close his eyes and clear his mind. It was a meditation of sorts, heightening his focus and hardening his resolve. If he was to bring his sister home safely, then distractions must be done away with and he'd been much distracted lately.

It was just his luck that Anna's head fell against his shoulder right then. Pen looked down to find her sleeping, and the urge to wrap his arm around her and hold her close overtook him.

Since there appeared to be a perpetual battle raging inside him, the temptation to remove her and scoot to the side or even relocate to the seat opposite clashed with the need to hold her.

And neither won, for he remained in his position, stiff and tightly wound.

"ANNA," HE CALLED SOFTLY.

"Hmmm?" She snuggled closer.

He could allow her to sleep longer—and he wanted to—but he was exhausted and famished.

"Anna, wake up," he called again, this time giving her shoulder a little nudge.

"Are we home?" she asked, stretching beside him.

"We are." He disembarked and handed her from the carriage before walking up the short steps to the front door of Wrexford House.

"I'll come for you tomorrow. If we leave at seven, we should be there close to eight."

She nodded as the door was opened by the butler. It appeared as though he'd been watching for them. Without thinking, he picked up her gloved hand and raised it to his lips. "Be sure to eat something before you retire for the night," he said, kissing her knuckles.

Instead of climbing back into the carriage to be

taken home, he opted to walk. The light rain, the damp, leaf-littered Beacon Street, and the heavy fog that had settled, tempted him to continue walking down to Boston Common, the park that delighted the Brahmins during the day and became creepy at night. But he had to at least try to get some sleep. And he needed to eat.

Much like the Wrexford butler, Antoine opened the door before he could lift the heavy brass knocker.

"How is my mother?" he asked as Antoine took his coat and hat.

"She has remained in her chamber all day. Dr. Poole was by to see her in the afternoon. She complained of a bad headache."

"How is she now?" he asked, tugging his leather gloves loose.

"I believe she is asleep."

He nodded. "And my sister?"

"She had Lady Caroline over until after dinner. She is still aware of nothing seriously amiss."

"Good." He made for the staircase. "Get me something to eat," he called over his shoulder.

Pen strode down the hallway of the third floor, past his chambers to his mother's. The door opened soundlessly on well-oiled hinges and he stepped in. The rooms were gravely silent save for the echoes of his mother's even breathing as she slept. He nodded, satisfied that she was fine, and strode downstairs to his study. He was crossing the room toward the banked fire when a movement caught his eye. On closer inspection, he found Treacle, Mary's entitled brown cat, on the hearth rug. The animal opened one amber eye that caught the light and shone like an ominous jewel, then the other, and stared at Pen, presumably expecting him to fawn over it as everyone else did.

When it didn't get the attention it wanted, it stretched with languid abandon and rolled a few times, purring. That trick did not work either, and it slowly wagged its tail before rubbing itself on his leg.

He didn't understand this sudden show of affection; the only thing Treacle loved more than hissing at him was a herring meal. Either it was growing old and demented, or it was planning something sinister. Pen had great cause to believe the latter given how many times he'd been scratched in the past.

Antoine returned soon with a tray laden with a cold repast, which he lay on the small table between the two wingback chairs in front of the fireplace.

"Feed this thing. I don't like it following me," he ordered, giving Treacle a sidelong glance.

Antoine tried to pick up the cat and it hissed, extending a clawed paw in his direction and making him retreat.

Pen glared at both cat and butler. They were getting in the way of his mealtime.

"Leave it."

Antoine bowed and walked out of the room. Pen watched the cat warily as he unbuttoned his vest and rolled his shirtsleeves up to his elbows. It was eyeing the assortment of meats on the tray. Picking up a paper-thin slice of ham, he dangled it in front of the feline and when it would stretch to collect it, he would pull away once or twice before relinquishing the meat to the cat. They repeated this game several times before he began tending to his own stomach.

Roast beef, ham, pickles, and cheese on bread was just what he needed, and bite after bite, he finished everything on the tray, with Treacle's help, of course. He poured himself some tea and creamed it, pausing to give the cat some milk in a saucer, and he had just taken a large sip when a cold accusing voice stopped him short.

CHAPTER NINE

"Where were you all day?" Mary stood in the doorway, obviously seething. She was in her nightgown, her feet were bare and her dark hair down. "Mama needed you today. Where were you?"

"I was out running some errands," he replied, setting his teacup down and leaning back in his chair.

"Of course you were," she scoffed. "Mama was unwell. When I couldn't find you, I sent for Libby. I was told she and Anna were not in."

He clenched his jaw.

"I know something is going on. I can sense it in the hushed whispers." Mary stepped into the room.

Pen didn't know what to tell her. On the one hand, he didn't want to alarm her with news of

Libby's disappearance, and on the other, he wanted her to know the truth should the worst come to pass.

"What is going on, Penforth?"

He sighed. *Out with it. It's better this way*, he thought. "Libby is missing."

"What?" She blanched and her brown eyes pooled with sudden tears.

"She disappeared two days ago from Anna's soirée." Pen was trying to break this to her as gently as he could, but she was not taking it well.

"And what are you doing to find her?" Her expression was both horrified and accusing. There was no uncertainty as to who she blamed.

"Everything I can."

"I don't believe you. I don't trust you're doing everything you can to find my sister."

"She's my sister too," he reminded her. "And I have been out with Anna all day looking for her. All last night and the night before, too." He disliked the desperate tone he detected in his own voice. "You have to believe me."

The pain and lack of faith were clear in her eyes. "Why should I? You've never cared about us."

The accusation stung. "I have always ensured that you have a roof over your head," he said coolly. "You eat well, you move in the best circles, and you wear the latest and most expensive fashion." He took a breath to uncoil the agitation from his mind. "Don't tell me I don't care."

"You're barely here!" she snapped, sinking into the other chair and dropping her face into her hands. "If you'd been here for us, if you'd been watching us, Libby wouldn't have disappeared."

"I was at the soirée," he said defensively.

The sixteen-year-old shook her head. "That's even worse!"

With a choking feeling in his throat, he leaned forward to touch her shoulder but she shrunk from him.

"Mary..."

She began to sob.

"I'll find Libby. I promise you that."

"Your promises mean nothing." She stood up and fled the room. Treacle followed moments later.

Pen raked his fingers through his hair and groaned. The feeling of failure was keen and heavy. He would rest tonight, rebuild his strength and energy, and then on the morrow, he and Anna would return to Cambridge and move heaven and earth to find Libby.

THE QUIET AND GLOOM THAT GREETED ANNA UPON entry into her home was almost crushing. Webb's grim demeanor further darkened the house.

"Did anyone come looking for me?" She asked the question half-heartedly, not because she'd particularly been expecting anyone.

"Yes, my lady." Webb adjusted his starched neckcloth before he continued. "Princess Mary Armstrong-Leeds sent for you and her sister."

"Oh, no," Anna breathed, dread mixing with guilt.

"I saw to it that she was informed you were both out."

Mary had not seen or heard from Libby for a while; she must know by now that something was wrong. Anna didn't want to face her until they had found Libby. What could she possibly say? Yes, she didn't have any control over that night's events, but it had happened in her house, thus making the responsibility hers.

"Is there anything else?"

"I don't believe there is, my lady. Unless we are going to count the pile of invitations and missives waiting for your response." He waved toward the envelopes littering the marble console against the left wall of the entrance hall.

She dismissed them with a wave of her hand.

Everything would have to wait until her best friend was found.

"Have Eva run me a bath, and I would like something to eat…something warm."

She clutched the polished balustrade and lifted her heavy skirt to begin a weary procession up the stairs.

It didn't take long for Eva to have a bath ready and while helping Anna out of her dress, the maid nervously cleared her throat. Then she did it again. Anna thought nothing of it until she did it a third time.

"Is something wrong with your throat?"

"Err…forgive what I am about to say, my lady." She paused and Anna waited patiently. "There is some talk in the servants' quarters."

Anna knew what talk it was and she was not surprised. It was bound to come out, eventually. "Talk of what?"

Eva hesitated.

"You can tell me, Eva."

"It's Lady Elizabeth. Some of the servants are talking of a disappearance."

"I see," she said coolly, contemplating whether to have a staff meeting this night or wait until morning.

"Mr. Webb has given us all a censure and asked

us to be quiet about it," she quickly clarified, correctly interpreting Anna's stern look.

"In that case, I will see all of you in the morning." She trusted Webb, but felt she needed to add to his efforts in keeping Libby's disappearance a secret. Well, it was not much of a secret now, was it?

"There is something else you should know," Eva said.

Anna was about to step into her bath but she stood, waiting to Eva to continue.

"The footman Robert told me he saw the new footman Van Daal speaking with a strange man in the garden that night."

Anna's eyes widened at the news. "Did he tell you what the strange man looked like?"

"Yes, he had the look of a hired ruffian; bald and brawny."

"Get Robert," Anna ordered, grabbing the thick velvet dressing gown Eva had laid out for her on the bed.

"Now?" Eva asked.

On second thought, she would have that staff meeting right now. "Tell Webb to summon everyone to the rose drawing room."

"Yes, my lady." Eva scurried out of the room, tripping and almost falling as she went.

If Robert was right, then Libby's abduction had

inside involvement. This had to be dealt with without delay. She couldn't believe one of the servants would do this, but then, *that* particular staff member was new.

They were waiting for her with wary and perplexed expressions on their faces when she reached the drawing room.

"I believe you are aware of what happened in this house. The issue involving my friend, Princess Elizabeth."

Some nodded while others remained impassive. The new footman was one of the impassive ones.

"I should have questioned all of you that night, but I will admit the thought did not occur to me. Do you know why I didn't think to question you?" Her gaze roamed their faces, one after the other. "Because I trust you." Her eyes were on Webb and the housekeeper Mrs. Faulkner when she said that. Mrs. Faulkner lowered her eyes in obvious embarrassment.

She was placing some blame on them. Perhaps it was unfair, but they were tasked with employing new staff. If they could not do that properly, then she had every cause to believe they did not have her family's best interests at heart.

"I need anyone who knows *anything* about this matter, to step forward."

Eva nervously stepped out from the line, giving Robert a knowing look. After a moment, he too stepped out. Everyone else remained where they were.

"Anyone else?" Anna asked. No additional person stepped forward. "Fine. All of you with the exception of Van Daal, Eva, Robert, Webb, and Mrs. Faulkner may leave."

Van Daal tugged at his neckcloth—a clear indication of his guilt—as the others filed out of the drawing room.

"Eva, please repeat what you said to me upstairs."

Furtively casting an anxious glance in Van Daal's direction, Eva cleared her throat and reiterated what she had told Anna.

"Can you confirm that, Robert?"

Robert nodded. "Yes, my lady."

She turned to Van Daal, who was now sweating. "Are they telling the truth?"

He did not respond.

"You are being spoken to, boy," Webb said in a chilly voice.

"Y-yes, m-my lady," he stammered.

Her hands balled into fists at her side as she tried to keep her voice even. "Who put you up to it?"

"William Singer. I knew him from my youth. He gave me money—I really needed the money—and asked me to watch Lady Elizabeth. To inform him as soon as she was alone."

Anna bit the inside of her cheek in anger. "How much did he give you?"

"Fifteen dollars." He bowed his head in what looked like shame.

"I see fifteen dollars is more important than your job, reputation, and security."

"Forgive me, my lady. I should never have done that." He sank to his knees.

"Of course you would say that after getting caught. Where is Singer now?

"I don't know." His chin quivered and it further angered Anna. He had sold her family for fifteen dollars! Truculence and violence were not in her nature, but she wanted to hit him right then. "I know where he lives," the man added.

Without being asked, Webb retrieved a paper and a pen from the escritoire. "The address?" he demanded. Van Daal obeyed and Webb wrote it down and handed her the sheet.

"Do you have any family?" she asked.

"No. I am an only child and my folks are dead."

Not having any family should make what she was going to do easier. "Find somewhere to lock him up tonight. The police will come for him in the morning," she said to Webb and Mrs. Faulkner.

Van Daal lay flat, grasping at the skirt of her robe, begging, but she stepped away. Webb caught the man's flailing arms and, with Robert's help, bound them behind him with the neckcloth he'd been wearing.

If Pen had been here, he'd have throttled Van Daal. Maybe luck was real. This man had gotten lucky.

Anna sank onto the nearest sofa and Mrs. Faulkner sidled up to her. "I am so sorry, dear child."

Anna wanted to cry. "I don't know how this happened, Mrs. Faulkner."

"He had several excellent recommendations. We really thought he was good."

Perhaps she was wrong to blame them for hiring a bad apple. Good recommendations often validated employers' trust and they obviously thought they could trust Van Daal. "It's not your fault."

"We shall be more strict and run more background checks in future, I promise you," Mrs. Faulkner assured.

"Thank you, Mrs. Faulkner." She stood. Her bath must have gone cold by now.

The older woman gave Anna a motherly smile. "Eva will see that your bath is reheated, and I will be up with your dinner."

After a hot bath, Anna sat on her bed with her legs tucked under her and a food tray in front of her, willing herself to eat. She *had* been hungry earlier, but after the exhausting interrogation of the servants, she was too drained to muster any appetite. Nevertheless, she forced herself to eat the beef stew and the peach cobbler. Although the food was delicious enough to make her forget her pangs of hunger, it did nothing in the way of providing emotional comfort.

And when she lay her head on the pillow and pulled the cover over her head, the tears that had stung at the back of her eyes all day fell unbidden.

Once again, the cold claws of loneliness wrapped around her heart, crushing it. Every tear that fell yearned to be wiped away by a loving hand.

She wished Libby had never disappeared. She wished her mother was home. She wished Pen could see her as more than Libby's friend. Her time with him today had sparked a realization; opened her mind to feelings she didn't know had been growing. And now the thought of those feelings going unrequited was quite unbearable.

WHEN ANNA WOKE IN THE MORNING, SHE WAS STILL tired, as if she'd run several miles, but her mind was sharp and clear. She had a task to do.

She swung her feet to the side of the bed and peered at the clock on the dresser: it was just past six. Wrapping herself in her robe, she stood and walked to the window where she pulled the heavy velvet drapes apart to let some light into the room. A mist-covered garden that had completely succumbed to the draining powers of Fall greeted her. And the ash tree she loved sitting under was almost devoid of leaves.

Was anything cheery anymore?

She turned from the window and crossed the room to ring for Eva.

Knowing where they would be venturing today, she chose a dress of gray velvet. A melancholic color, she knew, but also inconspicuous. And when she was dressed, she went downstairs to arrange to send a message to Penforth.

He'd said he would come for her at seven but things had changed. There was Van Daal to deal with.

Although the house had long been awake, the sound of her boot heels clicking against the parquet floor and the ticking of the grandfather clock in the foyer were the only audible sounds. The feeling of desertion once more rose to the surface, but before it could take hold, Mrs. Faulkner appeared.

"Good morning, child," she greeted with forced cheer.

"Good morning, Mrs. Faulkner," Anna returned. "I need to send a message to Sir Penforth as soon as possible. And, please have my breakfast ready. I will be in the dining room shortly."

"Of course. I'll fetch a messenger."

Anna proceeded to her father's private sanctum and sat in the leather chair behind the massive lacquered mahogany desk. She found a paper and a pen and scrawled a message for Pen. The footman who would deliver the message entered as she was applying the wax seal to the envelope.

"Take this directly to Sir Penforth and wait for a reply."

He bowed before leaving. Anna was rising from the chair when a persistent knock echoed through the house. She picked up her skirts and rushed out into the foyer. The person attacking the front door did not put the knocker down, for they continued to slam it against the door without rest.

Looking as unperturbed as could be, Webb crossed the hall and opened the door. Before he or

Anna had time to register the person on the other side, a small figure in blue pushed past Webb and made straight for Anna.

Her arms shot out with lightning speed to hold off the figure—a girl.

The girl lowered the hood of her cloak.

"Mary?" Anna gasped, surprised.

"Is it true?" the young girl asked. Her eyelids were red and swollen from crying.

"Oh, dear." She pulled Mary into her arms. "Come and sit."

Taking her into the rose drawing room, she lowered her onto the sofa and divested her visitor of her damp cloak.

"Has Libby truly gone missing?" she asked, as Anna sat beside her.

A nod was the only confirmation she could give and the girl burst into tears.

Anna gathered her close, cooing softly to comfort her.

"We're doing everything we can to find her. Pen—"

Mary pulled away quickly and her dark eyes turned hard. "Don't talk to me about Pen! This is all his fault!"

Anna had a feeling there was more to Mary's accusation than met the eye.

"If it's anyone's fault, it's mine, Mary. Libby was in this house, under *my* care when she disappeared. Pen had nothing to do with it."

She shook her head. "It's not your fault, Anna. Pen has never paid attention to us. Who we *are*, how we *feel*."

"But that is no reason to blame him."

Her dark expression was directed at Anna now. "Are you defending him?"

"I am not taking anyone's side," Anna said in a mollifying tone. "I understand the issues you have with your brother and I don't want them to obstruct your judgment. He is doing everything he can to bring Libby back."

"I don't trust he is doing everything he can." Mary shot to her feet and began pacing the room. "He hardly ever talks to me or Libby, or even Mama. We're nothing but people sharing the same house and for whom he is duty-bound to provide."

Anna understood the neglect Mary was feeling, for Libby had often expressed similar sentiments about her brother. And yet, she also understood Pen's detachment. He'd once held something dear and it had been taken from him. He didn't want to lose again, and his way of protecting himself had been to keep his distance, from everyone and everything.

"Mary," Anna walked up to the young girl and halted her pacing by taking her hands. "You're Pen's family and he cares deeply for you. He merely has a hard time showing his feelings."

The girl sniffed as her chin quivered. "You think so?"

Anna wanted to believe it. "I know so," she said firmly. "Have you taken a good look at him since the start of this unfortunate event?"

Mary shook her head.

"He's neither slept nor eaten properly. We were out all day yesterday and in a short while we will be gone again, likely for the whole day today, too. We won't rest until Libby is home safe."

Mary hugged her tightly. "I am just so scared."

"I know, sweetheart. Everything will be fine."

Anna was scared too, but she couldn't admit that. Mary needed someone to be strong and Anna was going to be that person.

"Come, let's have breakfast. You must be hungry." She pulled away and offered Mary a clean handkerchief from her dress pocket.

"Yes," Mary replied, cleaning her eyes and nose.

They walked arm in arm to the dining room where Mrs. Faulkner had breakfast waiting.

"How is your mother?" Anna asked as she took a seat.

"I have not seen her this morning, but she was doing better last night after the physician's visit. She is not taking this well." Mary reached for some toast and jam.

"Understandably." Anna gratefully accepted a mug of chocolate from Mrs. Faulkner and began adding milk and sugar. "I will see her again as soon as I can."

A sip of the warm chocolate and a piece of toast calmed her nerves. The warmth of the liquid flowing down her throat into her stomach gave her some comfort, though the effect was far too brief.

"Where are you going today? And where did you go yesterday?" Mary bit into her toast with a loud crunch.

Anna felt she should leave out some details so as not to further upset the girl. "We are following a lead. A place in Cambridge...a carriage crossroads, to be exact."

"Can I come with you?"

"I am sorry, but that's impossible. It's not altogether safe."

"I can't sit here and do nothing," she whined.

"Christiana needs you, now more than ever. That will be more help than anything, in the situation."

She paused as if considering Anna's words. "You're right. I should be with my mother."

Anna smiled and gave her hand a reassuring squeeze.

"Good advice," an unmistakable voice drawled from the doorway.

CHAPTER TEN

The catch in her breath, the flutter in her stomach and the clenching in her chest were entirely unexpected. Anna never thought that one person—one *man*—could arouse such feelings, and all at once.

Penforth was a sight in a dark gray coat, matching trousers, and a black vest that fit his form with sartorial perfection. His black hair was damp, either from a bath or the light rain outside.

His color choice matched hers, but then, he always dressed in dark colors.

As he walked into the room, Anna noticed he favored his healthier leg, and his face held a grimace when he sat in the chair opposite theirs.

"Mary," he greeted gently.

"Penforth," she returned, avoiding his eyes.

Tension thickened the air, making Anna very uncomfortable, like a cord had been wound tight about her.

"What would you like?" she asked Pen. "Coffee, tea, or chocolate?"

"Coffee would be fine." He picked up a slice of toast and began buttering, a question burning in his eyes; impeded by his sister's presence.

Anna signaled for the footman to serve coffee. She was dying to occupy herself, to avoid the pull of Pen's presence.

"Anna told me the two of you will be heading out to continue the search for Libby," Mary said.

Very briefly, his affection for his sister shone in his eyes before it was concealed by a cloud of indifference. Affected indifference. "Yes, we'll leave shortly."

She nodded. "I judged you too harshly. I am sorry," she said quietly after a moment, her eyes glued to her half-eaten toast.

Anna smiled to herself. Mary was reaching out, extending the proverbial olive branch. It was up to Pen now to accept it and repair their relationship.

"I should be apologizing to you for being so aloof all these years."

"You're making amends now, aren't you?"

"I'm trying."

She finally looked up at that, and gave him a tentative smile. He returned it with one of his own. Anna felt a sense of pride, as if she had somehow played a hand in their truce.

When they finished eating, Pen stood, circled the table, and held out his hand to Anna.

"There's some business we have to take care of before we leave," he explained to his sister.

"I shall go see if Mama has woken."

"Yes, good idea." Pen pulled Anna to her feet. The gesture, coupled with his strong masculine energy, warmed her cheeks and called to the fore those feelings of affection swirling inside her.

To get away from him and the emotions, she pulled Mary out of the dining room and back to the drawing room to retrieve her cloak.

"Eva will accompany you home," she said, helping the girl adjust the heavy wool about her shoulders. "I don't want you out by yourself again. It's not safe."

"I won't do it again." Mary's expression softened. "Thank you, Anna. For everything."

Anna pulled her into her arms. "Always. I see you as family."

Mary pulled away with something like an impish grin on her face. "Are you and Pen…?"

Anna shook her head. "No. We're not."

The young girl sighed. "That's a shame, for I would love to have you as a second sister."

So would Anna, but she didn't want to dwell on impossibilities now. She had too much to think about and much to do.

"Give my best to Christiana."

After Anna had seen Mary off, Webb approached. "Mr. Graves is here, my lady. He waits in the blue drawing room."

"What's going on?" Pen asked, his impatience palpable.

In her note, she'd made mention of a new development in Libby's case without going into detail. She'd also asked Pen to send for Mr. Graves.

"One of our footmen, Van Daal, was ostensibly hired by a man named William Singer to watch Libby," she explained, and saw his expression turn murderous.

"Where is he now?" Pen asked through clenched teeth.

"Detained in the cellar, sir," Webb replied.

"Show me." He turned to follow Webb and Anna grabbed his arm.

"Pen, wait. Don't be rash."

He yanked his arm from her grasp, the hardness in his gaze now directed at her. "You think me a heedless brute."

"I—"

"You think I am going down there to beat him up."

He was right to some degree; a part of her thought he'd throttle Van Daal on sight. But Pen was not a violent man, despite his possession of a mercurial temper.

"Get Graves," he commanded over his shoulder.

She led the puzzled police officer to the cellar and remained by the doorway at the top of the stairs, watching the scene unfold. It appeared Pen had already questioned the man.

"Take him away and lock him up," Pen said to Mr. Graves.

"May I ask the reason you want him locked up, sir?"

"Tell him," he ordered Van Daal.

"I was hired by William Singer to watch Lady Elizabeth and report her movement on the night she disappeared." He sounded sullen now, and had a belligerent look in his eye. Clearly, a night in the cellar had not shown him the error of his ways.

The police officer nodded, and heaved the man to his feet and up the stairs. Anna stepped aside to let them through.

"Perhaps you were right and the lady truly was

abducted." Grave whispered to Anna as he passed, his eyes darting in Pen's direction. The man at least possessed enough wit to be aware of the dangers of speaking to Pen about this. "Shall we resume the investigation, Your Grace?"

"I am not the one you should be asking."

Pen joined them. "Why are you tarrying?" he asked Mr. Graves.

"Nothing, si—"

"Mr. Graves was just suggesting he resume the investigation."

Pen gave an intimidating smile. "Oh, you want to help now?"

"Yes, of course."

Pen looked as if he was about to censure the officer, but changed his mind and instead said simply, "Search for Singer. The duchess and I will return to Cambridge shortly to question a carriage driver named Arthur Pelham. He might have a lead about Lady Elizabeth."

Mr. Graves bowed. "Forgive me for doubting this case, sir."

Pen's upper lip curled derisively. "Get to work." He looked down at Anna. "I am certain you're pleased I've not pulverized the footman's face."

"It was wrong of me to make such assumptions. I am sorry."

He shrugged and brushed past her.

PEN PONDERED WHAT ANNA HAD SAID TO MARY TO calm her down. She was not the easiest girl to deal with and that was one of the reasons he avoided her. After last night, he didn't think she'd ever speak to him again, but she had…and even apologized.

He turned his gaze from the carriage window to the woman in front of him. He could ask her what she'd said, but that would be admitting his own failure.

As though she felt his gaze on her, she raised her blue eyes to his.

"Nothing," he answered her silent question.

She turned to look at the passing scenery. They'd hardly spoken since the beginning of their journey more than half an hour ago. The pattern of their communication puzzled him. Sometimes it appeared they were friends and could talk about anything and everything; and sometimes, the air around them seemed wound tight with tension. He didn't know which of them was responsible for such inconsistencies.

Something was happening between them. There was no denying it. And the sooner they confronted it the better. He wanted to know what she thought of him and where he stood in her life. He'd occasionally caught her looking at him with something akin to fondness in her eyes. Pen couldn't let her continue to harbor such feelings. Not for him.

There was no room for romance in his life.

"What's on your mind?" he asked.

"I am not at liberty to share that with you," she replied, shifting slightly in her seat.

"They're thoughts of me, then," he declared with a smirk.

The blue flame in her eyes began to stir. "Why would I be thinking of you at this time?"

"Why not? We're alone in a carriage."

"Are you always this egocentric?"

He shrugged and then leaned forward to prop his elbows on his knees. "Something is happening between us. I can feel it."

Her gaze dropped to her hands on her lap. "I don't believe I understand your meaning."

"If I proposed marriage to you, would you accept?"

She appeared to take affront at the question. "What?"

"Would you accept?" he asked again. He was not sure where he was going with this. It didn't matter, as long as they got him the answers he wanted.

"No," she snapped.

"Why not?"

"We would not suit."

"I am not asking you whether we would suit or not. I am asking whether you could ever see me as your husband."

She sighed. "Fine. I have several reasons why not."

He leaned back in his seat and folded his arms. "Go on."

She began ticking off on her fingers. "Point the first: I am not in want of a husband. Point the second: your brooding would drive me to distraction. Point the third: you don't consider me your equal, and if you can't do that, then you can never truly respect me. Point the fourth: you are not romantic."

He'd hoped for rejection, so why now did her answer sting this much? He had thought he didn't want her to want him. Apparently, he didn't know *what* he wanted.

"And how do you feel about me despite these reasons?"

He caught a shadow in the depth of her eyes before she quickly recovered and shut him out.

"We're here," she said as the carriage rolled to a halt.

He was not done with this conversation.

They headed straight for the cluster of carriages where they'd spoken with Clayton yesterday. True to his word, he was waiting for them when they arrived, despite the fact that the Van Daal incident had made them somewhat later than expected. He removed his cap, revealing a greying bald head and tapped the tall, thin man next to him.

"Sir, I did as you asked. This is Arthur Pelham."

"Thank you, Clayton," Pen said, handing him a wad of money.

His eyes bulged out in surprise. "T-thank you!"

Pen turned his attention to Pelham who looked at him with distrust. "Did he give you our message?"

"Yes," the man replied warily. "Said I'll be in trouble if I don't wait for you."

"Yes, you could be if you don't comply. Can we step aside, please?" They moved away from Clayton and the other drivers.

"We're looking for two people you may have transported two days ago. This woman." He showed Libby's portrait. "And a man with light hair and a scar on his temple."

Pelham nodded. "Ah, yes, I remember them. A

very pretty girl and a very handsome man. I conveyed them some days ago. They were going to be wed."

Pen felt an icy chill run through him. He could not believe Libby would marry that easily and without any word to anyone. At twenty-two, and a year younger than Anna, Libby had stated she would never marry. He'd spent the better part of four years trying to persuade her otherwise, to no avail.

"The lady looked worse for wear and very drunk." Pelham chuckled. "I don't blame her. I mean, who wouldn't drink to celebrate their upcoming wedding? She must have been happy to be marrying the gentleman."

"This can't be true, Pen," Anna whispered. "Libby would never get married in such a manner. Not without telling me."

"I know," he murmured, his hand finding hers and holding tight. "Where did you take them?"

"I took them to Lexington."

"You're going to take us there," Pen said.

"I will be happy to take you, but I have passengers…" Pelham scratched his head and Pen got the sense that he wanted to bargain. He was looking to gain from this.

"Which one is your carriage?"

"That one." He pointed at the shabbiest carriage in the cluster.

"Do you have passengers waiting inside?"

He shook his head.

"Good. *We* are your passengers now. You don't have to worry about payment. You will gain from both the information you've given us and by taking us to Lexington."

The man's eyes sparkled capriciously as he motioned for them to follow him to his carriage. Pen put a hand on his shoulder to stop him. There was no way he was going to allow Anna to ride in a carriage like that. She was not just any lady born with privilege, she was a duchess. And a good friend of his family.

And what is she to *you?* His mind's voice asked.

No, he would not go there. Not now.

"We will follow you in *our* carriage," he said to Pelham.

The man shrugged. "Whatever pleases you, sir."

After handing Anna into his own carriage, he walked back to Pelham. He could have just instructed the man to ride beside his own driver and footman, but he felt this way was better.

"Stay close," he said, before handing over some coin. It was enough to light the man's eyes and ensure his cooperation. "You will receive more when we reach our destination."

"Yes, sir!" Pelham grinned.

Pen rejoined Anna and knocked on the roof of the carriage to signal the driver to get moving.

"Do you believe that bit about Libby marrying?" Anna asked. She seemed very worried.

"I don't know." He ran his fingers through his hair. "She seemed receptive to Sir Anthony, based on those letters."

"But she would never marry him, not like that. I know Libby and—"

"You have a pact," he finished for her.

Her mouth fell open.

"How do I know about it?" He shrugged. "I overheard you making promises to each other to die as spinsters if you don't find men who support your cause for indepedence."

She pressed her pretty lips together and glared at him. He smiled at how delectable she looked. Flushed with anger? Embarrassment? It didn't matter which. She was stunning and he could not fathom what she was doing to his mind. One moment he thought her obstinate to the point of exhaustion, and the next, he wanted to dance with her in the moonlight.

Dance with her in the moonlight? What was that about?

"Finding such men is an ordeal. Perhaps even more trouble than it's worth," she argued, drawing him out of his foolish thoughts.

"Oh, but it appears Sir Anthony supports her cause. He said so in his last letter."

Her cheeks took on a bloom. This time it could definitely be annoyance.

"That is still not enough reason for Libby to do something like this voluntarily."

"Because you know my sister so well." He meant for that statement to provoke her and it worked.

"Are you so desperate to marry her off that you are not abhorred by the notion of her marrying a man who abducted her?" She raised her voice a notch.

"Are you so insecure that you do not want to become a spinster alone? That the idea of your best friend getting married *willingly* and leaving you is unthinkable?"

The broken look in her eyes told him he'd hit a nerve and perhaps stepped out of line.

"You have no right to say that," she ground out.

"You're right. I apologize." And he truly was sorry.

"Is it bad to want something better for her? You look like you would not be too bothered if she married Sir Anthony."

"Don't misunderstand me, Anna."

"Then explain yourself," she seethed.

"The heart of a woman is malleable. That man could easily make her fall in love and want to marry him by presenting himself in the image of her dream. Most women have dreams," he held up a silencing finger, "and don't tell me that Libby is different. I may not know much about her, but I've seen drawings she made as a child; of herself being rescued from a monster by a prince, receiving flowers from an admirer, dancing with an admirer. I've seen them all. She had fantasies."

Anna looked away like a petulant child. "I've never seen those drawings." She folded her arms across her chest. "She could very well have outgrown them."

"You may be right. She could have, but I need you to keep an open mind." He took her hand and said gently, "I want my sister to be married but not to just any man. If we are too late and she has married this scoundrel, I promise you I will do everything I can to have the situation annulled."

Her chin quivered and her eyes glistened with tears. "I just want her to be all right."

Pen moved across to her seat and pulled her into his arms, running his hand up and down her back in a soothing motion. "I want that too, more than anything." She sniffed and his heart twisted, monumentally surprising him.

He didn't want to make Anna cry.

Tightening his arms around her, he said, "I truly didn't mean to upset you."

She didn't respond, causing him to pull away to look at her face. She was scrupulously trying to keep the tears in her eyes from spilling. Very gently, he took her face in both his hands and pressed his lips to her eyes, causing them to close and the tears to spill. He pulled away to wipe the wetness off her soft cheeks.

"Don't hold them in. Let them flow. I am here," he whispered.

"You should take your own advice," she said as more tears streamed down her cheeks.

He smiled a little as his heart twisted again. "I don't need to cry."

"But you need to release your pent-up emotions."

"Perhaps you're right." He lowered his head until their lips were a mere hairsbreadth apart. Closing his eyes, he let their closeness fill his senses; her lovely scent—lavender—her warm breath against his lips, the feeling of her in his arms. Despite the torrent of emotions raging inside him, he felt comfort.

Tenderly, Pen brushed his lips against her cheek, then traced the line of her jaw to her ear. A very subtle exotic scent arrested his nose and his nostrils flared in response. Kissing the tender spot below her ear caused her to shiver, sending waves of sensual echoes through him. Her hand came up to stroke his cheek and the feel of her soft fingers against his stubble-roughened cheek was almost too much to bear, so he pulled away and looked into the cerulean depths of her eyes.

He wanted to kiss her thoroughly, he truly did, but he was suddenly afraid of doing so.

hen Pen pulled away, Anna silently screamed at the bereavement. He stared into her eyes for a long moment, unblinking. It was as though he'd seen something fearful, and the icy tentacles of insecurity snaked up to grab her senses. Unable to bear his regard any longer, she closed her eyes and turned away, scooting to the other end of the seat.

Her movement seemed to pull him out of his daze and he blinked several times before clearing his throat. "Forgive me," he said hoarsely. "I shouldn't have done that. I shouldn't have taken such liberties."

Anna had never been more embarrassed in her life. Here she had thought he was starting to feel something for her. But just like last time, he seemed to be filled with regret. What was worse, was that she had fallen off the edge and into the unknown. Whether or not she examined her true feelings, her heart was already breaking and there was nothing she could do to stop it.

She failed to understand why he would initiate that sort of intimacy only to snuff out the light. Was she so very repulsive? Or was he that cold-hearted?

Rapidly blinking her tears away, she reached into her purse and retrieved Libby's diary. It was the only book she had with her and she was in desperate want of employment. Something to divert her mind from matters of her own heart.

Her trembling fingers found a page and she willed her eyes to look and her mind to read. It appeared to be an entry Anna had not seen before. Libby wrote about her mother's desire to have a grandchild, detailing the list of gentlemen she had her sights on for Libby, and those ladies who might be suitable for Penforth. Her own name was not on the latter list.

Anna snapped the small volume shut and let out a long slow breath. She could feel Pen's enigmatic gaze on her and she disliked it. She disliked a lot of things right now, especially being confined in this space.

"Stop the carriage, " she said stiffly.

"Why? Are you all right?"

"Just stop. Please."

He rapped on the carriage roof to signal the driver and a short stint later, they slowed to a halt. Before he could move, she swung the door open and hopped down, not even waiting for the small set of steps to be unfolded. She gathered her heavy skirts and began stalking toward Pelham's carriage which had stopped a short distance away.

"Anna!" Pen called, catching up to her. "What is the matter?"

"I should be asking *you* that," she ground out, not slowing her pace.

Taking hold of her arm, he forced her to stop and when she almost lost her balance, he caught her in his arms. She pried herself from his grip and gathered up her skirts again. The light rain was beginning to increase.

"Let's get back inside the carriage and you can tell me what is wrong," he said.

"I don't want to talk to you," she half-snapped. "And I don't want to ride in your carriage."

The skies rumbled in the distance before a large flash signaled an oncoming storm. Pen squinted up for a moment before looking back at her. "We need to get moving, Anna. We are not even halfway there and if this storm catches us on the road, we'll have a bigger complication to contend with than simply sharing a carriage."

"Fine, go back to your carriage and I will ride with Pelham."

"I would rather you ride in mine. I do not trust Pelham."

Frustration tightened her voice. "I don't want to argue with you." She continued walking.

"Your safety matters to me, Anna."

"Penforth, I don't care and I don't want to talk right now!"

He must have realized at last that arguing was futile, because he let her go. She did not look back to check whether he was still standing where she'd left him. Instead, she climbed up into Pelham's carriage without assistance and pulled the door closed before arranging her now-damp skirts about her.

Your safety matters to me. Did it really, though? She'd been stupid to let her heart soften toward him. His implication that she was selfish enough to not want Libby to marry so they could remain spinsters together should have given her enough warning to stay away. But her fluttery heart had yielded to his soft kisses and sensual caresses.

Resolving to steel herself and raise her guard back up, she turned to look out the window at the rain. The crash of thunder and the fingers of lightning that struck the sky made her recoil. She wrapped her arms around herself and looked nervously about the carriage interior.

It was a very old vehicle, several years out of fashion, but still seemed sturdy enough. The paint on the wood had all but faded and the seats creaked with every roll of the carriage wheels. As her eyes roamed the frayed red velvet covering the seats, she caught sight of a cream-colored piece of fabric sticking out from between the cushions.

Anna pulled it out to examine, and realized it was a ribbon from the dress Libby had initially planned to wear on the evening of the soirée. She knew the ribbon well, because Libby had borrowed the dress from Anna. In the end, she had settled instead on the emerald green because she thought it matched her hazel eyes better. Had Libby changed into this one when she went to her room that night? Anna fingered the cream organza, tracing the unique pattern of black embroidered swirls as she pondered.

She'd believed Pelham, of course, but the discovery of this dress piece confirmed his veracity as well as assured her that they were following the right trail. She searched the carriage interior for more clues but unfortunately came up empty.

Suddenly, there was a cracking sound. No sooner had the sound registered than she was thrown off her seat. There was a sharp pain in her head as she hit the opposite wall, and then nothing.

PENFORTH SAT UP, ALERT, AS SOON AS HE FELT THE carriage slow. Once it halted, he opened the door and stepped down. His blood froze in his veins at the sight of Pelham's turned-over carriage. He didn't stop to ask what had happened or why. He merely took flight toward the wreck.

Time slowed and his body quickened. His leg pain was forgotten as he raced toward Anna. It felt like an eternity. She was in there somewhere and she was probably hurt.

Pelham was struggling to heft his storky body up onto the carriage door which now faced up toward the sky, and at first glance, Pen saw the reason for the carriage turning over. The right back wheel had broken, presumably from a sudden descent into a ditch, and almost half the carriage was now sunken in the mire. In front, he could see the team struggling to stand but restrained by their harness. The horses could injure themselves if they continued pulling against their harness like that.

"Free the horses!" he shouted to Pelham before launching himself onto the carriage and wrenching at the door.

The weathered wood provided him with enough friction to heave himself to the top, but his weight began to sink the whole contraption more quickly into the mud-filled ditch. He had to act fast and get Anna out before the entire thing disappeared.

As he yanked at the door he almost got hit in the face when it opened more quickly than expected. Apparently, Anna had been on the other side trying to push the door open, fighting gravity.

She was afraid. He could see it in her wide eyes.

Planting his feet firmly, he bent down and reached for her.

"Hold onto my arms as tightly as you can," he instructed.

She did as he asked and he began pulling her up. Their collective weight, combined with the force they were exerting, caused the carriage to lurch and Pen almost lost his balance. She yelped and tightened her grip.

"I have you," he assured, his breath coming in rasps. "Hold on, Anna. I have you."

As soon as half her body was out, he quickly transferred his grip to her waist. Her freed arms came up about his shoulders and she held onto him tightly while he called for his driver to assist in carrying her down. She was shivering and looked much agitated when he climbed down after her. Without wasting any more time, he swept her up into his arms and over to his carriage.

It was when he was trudging through the wet road in the rain with her in his arms that he realized how angry he was. This would not have happened if she had remained with him, where he could *protect* her. But then he glanced down and found the anger ebbing away. Anna looked so small and fragile in his arms. He couldn't remain angry with her. He didn't want to.

"We are turning back and taking you home," he said after she was settled in the carriage.

"No!" she cried. "I am fine. I am not hurt anywhere."

"I would rather you're home. You'll be safer there."

"Not this again. I am fine, Penforth, and I insist we continue. Libby needs the two of us whether or not you choose to believe it."

This version of Anna—the one pressing him to continue his search for his sister with her—and the vulnerable Anna of moments ago were like two entirely different people.

"Are you certain?" he asked.

"Yes," she replied tightly. "We are running out of time, Pen."

She was right about time being against them, of course, but for some strange reason he had a feeling that she was not telling him the full truth.

"Fine."

He returned to Pelham, who'd successfully freed his horses and was circling his carriage, presumably trying to determine how to get it out of the ditch.

"We will continue the journey. You will sit with my driver and direct him," he said.

"With all due respect, sir, look at my carriage." He waved at the carnage. "How am I supposed to pull this thing out in this rain? Not to talk about the cost of repairing it. And look, one of my horses is limping."

Pen didn't have the patience for this man's complaining. "I'll buy you a new carriage." He raised his hand and motioned to his footman to come over. "How far are we from Lexington?"

"A couple of miles."

The wounded horse likely could not make the distance.

"Is there a small town or village in between?"

"We just left Arlington, sir."

"Do you think your horses can make it there?"

"Yes, sir."

He turned to the footman. "James, you will take the horses to Arlington. Find a new horse on which to ride back and meet us in Lexington."

"Right away, sir."

While James went to carry out his master's bidding, Penforth looked back at Pelham and asked, his voice laced with irony. "Will that be all?"

"Thank you very much, sir." The man bowed and hurried to take his new place beside the driver.

Pen climbed back into the carriage and they began moving again. Anna was hugging herself when he sat down. She must have left her cloak behind in the other carriage. He picked up his greatcoat that was thankfully dry and handed it to her. She wrapped the heavy wool about her and leaned back, closing her eyes.

The way she winced while leaning back, and the careful way she moved her head, told him the tale of what had happened when that carriage turned. It was apparent that Anna must have been hurt and was attempting to hide her pain. Perhaps it was foolish to allow her to continue the journey, but he silently resolved to take her home the moment she showed signs of worsening.

Reaching into his coat pocket, he pulled out a silver flask. He never went anywhere without it and it was hardly ever empty. He unscrewed the cap and passed the flask to her.

"Here. It will help warm you."

She took it and paused to admire the scrollwork around the flask before taking a cautious sip. "Whiskey," she said after swallowing.

"You don't like it?" He pulled off his gloves and placed them beside him before shrugging out of his wet afternoon coat and spreading it out on the seat next to the gloves.

"I do," she assured him. "Thank you." She took a couple more sips before passing it back.

Unlike her, he took a large swig, enjoying the trail of fire the liquid set as it flowed down his throat. He took another draft before putting the drink away. His eyes were on her throughout and he wondered if she was still upset with him. Being on the receiving end of her sharp tongue and blazing eyes felt better than watching her tightly clutch that coat to her as she fought to stay warm.

Cursing under his breath, he moved across to sit beside her, and tugged at the coat. "Give me your hands."

She did, and he removed her black leather gloves, then took her small icy hands in his and began rubbing them.

"You'll get warm quicker this way."

"This would not have happened if I had stayed here," she said quietly. "I am sorry."

He didn't say anything. He tried to pull her to him, and she winced.

"I...I may have hit my head," she confessed when he gave her a questioning look.

"Oh, God, Anna!" He sighed.

"You were going to send me home," she said almost sullenly.

"Only because I want you well."

"I am well enough. And the whiskey has helped." Her eyes were pleading.

"Come here." He pulled her to him, gentler this time—not that he'd been rough earlier. Eventually her steady breathing told him she'd fallen asleep, and he took the opportunity to place a soft kiss on the top of her head.

A heavy feeling settled in his heart as he held her. Somehow, he'd moved from watching Anna from a distance and keeping his thoughts and feelings to himself, to spending three full days in her company and allowing those feelings to grow. He'd convinced himself that he had his emotions in check. But as he held her now, he knew he had lost the battle in regard to how he felt about Duchess Wrexford, Lady Anna Trevallyn.

CHAPTER TWELVE

When she woke, the pain in her head had abated substantially. The liquor had worked quite well and Anna couldn't be more relieved. She'd been afraid Pen would send her home and she would miss out on finding her friend.

The comfortable—almost too comfortable—warmth around her reminded her that she was in Pen's arms. She'd *slept* in Pen's arms. She sighed, her emotions conflicted. Part of her wished she could remain here in the circle of his embrace forever.

"Are you awake?" he whispered.

She nodded but didn't move.

"How long have I been asleep?" She tried to nestle closer without him noticing, although she suspected he would. He was very observant.

"Half an hour or so." He sounded tired.

"I thought it was longer than that."

"How do you feel?" He looked down at her.

"Better. Much better."

He smiled. "Good. We're almost there."

Anna pulled away from him reluctantly and removed a small mirror from her purse. The purse she'd forgotten about when she stalked off in a huff earlier. Luckily it had stayed dry in Pen's carriage. Checking her reflection, she was glad she'd done her hair in a simple bun at her nape. Although it was somewhat mussed and damp, the damage was tolerable and almost presentable. She smoothed back the locks that had escaped and checked her face for any damage from the accident. All seemed to be as it should.

The carriage began to slow and Pen reached for his coat and hat. His bad leg was stretched out in front of him.

"You know, I've been meaning to ask why you do not carry a cane. Lots of fashionable gentlemen often do."

He turned to look at her, his surprise apparent. "Are you seriously asking that?"

She frowned. "I don't see why not. And, why should you not wish to answer?"

"Their legs are perfectly fine and so their use of a cane is not for function, but merely *fashionable*…"

He didn't complete his response. He didn't need to. The disgust in his tone at that last word spoke volumes.

"I thought a cane would help," she said softly, feeling guilty for bringing up such an obviously sensitive topic.

He sighed, somewhat dramatically, she thought. "Truth be told, it would. Having it relieve some weight from my leg would be excellent, but I don't want to use one. Walking is exercise, and movement is what the leg requires." His dark eyes met hers. "I had to teach myself to walk again, and spent many hours forcing my leg to not give up on me. I am better off without a cane."

Something had changed in him. The Pen she knew would have immediately become defensive and shut her out at the mention of a cane. And yet, here he was, explaining things to her.

"It was how I beat the odds. Exercise." He smiled then and she felt her eyes widen.

Where had this cooperative man come from? This was not Prince Penforth Armstrong-Leeds. If he was, then perhaps she'd not been the only one who hit her head.

The Armstrong-Leeds carriage rolled to a halt

and when she peeped out she saw they were in front of a chapel. At first glance, one would think the chapel ordinary. The stone walls and stained glass windows gave it a look like any other of its kind, but if this was where Libby had been delivered, then perhaps the building hid darker-than-usual secrets.

The rain had lessened to a drizzle, but the churning clouds above were still brewing a storm.

"You brought them to a chapel?" Anna asked Pelham once she and Pen had alighted.

"Told you they were getting married, my lady."

She shouldn't be surprised, and yet she was. Foreboding filled her.

"I know of this place," Pen said, his eyes dark and unreadable. "They call it the Blue Chapel of Lexington."

From his stern tone, Anna suspected the *blue* didn't stand for color.

"It is known amongst the less salubrious for collecting bribes and arranging hasty weddings," he confirmed, when she raised an enquiring brow.

Suddenly, Anna didn't want to go inside for fear of what they might find. The knowledge that this place hid behind a visor of holiness to cheat people further made her uncomfortable.

Pelham's happy murmurs of appreciation drew her attention off the chapel for a moment. Pen had paid him and from the way Pelham was grovelling, it must have been a generous amount. The carriage driver turned to Anna.

"Thank you, my lady. I wish you luck in finding your friend."

She inclined her head graciously. Whatever had happened to Libby was not the driver's fault.

Pen took her hand and started toward the chapel entrance. Her initial trepidation returned full force and she had to fight off a fit of the shakes.

The interior was quiet and dark. The sound of their boots on the stone floor echoed in the space as they walked down the aisle hand in hand.

As if the heavens were trying to tell them something, the rain chose that moment to pour down with a vengeance, loudly pelting the roof and windows. Lightning illuminated the nave and Anna's grip on Pen's hand tightened involuntarily.

A man wearing a black robe walked up to them, greeting them with a wide smile and a mercenary glint in his eyes.

"Welcome," he said, opening his arms as though he were about to embrace them. "I am Luke Anders, the minister here. How may I help you?"

"We are looking for a couple who may have married here in the past couple of days," Pen responded without returning the minister's greeting.

That made Mr. Anders's face fall. "Oh, I thought you were looking to be married yourselves."

"Why? Because that is all that ever goes on in this place?" Anna asked, annoyed.

"Of course not, my lady," he defended quickly. "May I ask who you are looking for?"

They provided Libby's portrait and the minister's eyes instantly flashed with recognition. "Ah yes," he nodded. "They were here only yesterday."

"Were they wed?" Anna quickly asked.

"Yes, they were indeed. And a lovely service it was, too."

Anna's heart skipped a beat. *They were too late!*

"Show us the register," Pen demanded. "We need proof."

Mr. Anders hesitated, causing Pen to repeat the question with more force.

"Are you with the police?" the minister asked. By now his earlier composure had cracked. He kept swallowing repeatedly.

Anna was tempted to answer yes but decided against it. There was no telling what this man might do. If he ran away; denied them further information...

"Yes," said Pen. "We are. I am Inspector Armstrong and this is my wife."

Anna's stomach tumbled into chaos. Had Pen gone mad, announcing her as his wife and making himself an inspector?

Mr. Anders's jaw dropped, and then snapped shut. "T-t-this way," he stammered, and led them to the south transept where a massive book lay open on a stand. "That is the register."

The volume was open to the newest entries and Anna leaned over to look. There, just above the latest entry, was Libby's marriage record.

Anna felt Pen lean in close behind her, and heard his sharp intake of breath. Libby's signature was clear. Not at all like someone under coercion, or the influence of drink.

"She's married," Pen whispered.

"She couldn't have married willingly. Pelham said she was intoxicated."

"That does not look like the signature of a drunk person." His voice was low and grave. Anna was afraid to look up and meet his eyes.

He was right. Libby's signature was very neat and elegant. It looked just like her usual cursive script.

"You said this place was corrupt. She could have been held at gunpoint."

Pen did not respond. He pointed at one of the witness names—William Singer.

The man who had hired someone to watch over her friend.

Anna turned sharply. "Mr. Anders..."

The minister was nowhere in sight. They rushed back to the nave. There was no sign of him.

Penforth unapologetically released a chain of expletives and Anna wanted to join him. Their next clue had just slipped through their fingers.

"He knows where she is," Pen said. His expression had moved past anger and was now in the realm of foreboding. "Otherwise, why run?" His body was rigid and his hands were balled into fists at his sides. "Let's go."

"Where are we going?"

"There is an inn across the road. We'll retire there and come up with a proper plan. The minister's reaction tells me we're close." His expression softened then. "And you need to dry your clothes and eat."

"So do you." Anna took a deep breath. "Pen, this is…" She couldn't finish. Her throat felt all choked up. Not only was Libby's reputation at risk, but Anna was more worried than ever for her friend's personal safety.

Pen nodded, grim-faced. "I know, Anna. We'll find her. I promise."

PRESENTING ANNA AS HIS WIFE WAS MUCH SIMPLER than presenting her as anything else. It gave him the opportunity to keep her close and protect her while respecting her reputation. They stepped across the road to the *Five Castles Inn.* The innkeeper, a pompous red-haired man, instantly took interest in their new guests. Their dishevelment had obviously done nothing to hide their social status and the innkeeper did not hide his desire to gain from this encounter.

The two rooms Pen requested were right beside each other, with an adjoining door as befitted a married couple. He asked Anna's permission first before accepting such a booking, though admittedly, she did not seem to be thinking very clearly at the moment. He did not want her by herself in an establishment such as this. Given her quick acquiescence with his plan, it was obvious she did not want to be too far from him, either.

She asked for a maid to be sent up to help dry her clothes.

"Will you be ready for dinner in an hour?" Pen asked when they reached her door.

"If my dress can be dried in time, yes."

"Hmm. I'll see you soon, then, Anna. Freshen

up, and then we will eat and decide our next steps. We're close. I feel it in my bones."

He found it curious that he was less bothered now by working with her, than he had been even a day or so earlier. Anna was clearly very intelligent and resourceful, and his concern for his sister overrode his natural instinct to keep Anna out of this for her own protection.

Oh, Libby, he thought, as his mind returned to his sister's signature on that book. *What have you gotten yourself into? And how are we going to extricate you from this?*

AFTER CLOSING THE DOOR BEHIND HER, ANNA stared around the bed chamber and sighed. Not out of any displeasure at the quality of the chamber—it was tolerable—but at the day she'd had. It was the most vexation she'd been through in one day, and the toll was great indeed.

Her left hand went up to massage her right shoulder where the joint was stiff and aching. She'd kept the full extent of her injuries from Pen, knowing what his reaction would have been. Apart from her head and right shoulder, she'd also hit her hip when the carriage had rolled. She was lost for some minutes in her musings, when a knock sounded at her door. It was accompanied by a shrill voice. "Housekeeping!"

"Come in!" Anna called, not feeling like answering the door herself.

A small blonde-haired girl entered and curtsied, as well as she could with a large box in her arms. "I was sent up to help you, ma'am."

"Ah, good. And what is that you're holding?"

"A dress for you, my lady."

"Wherever did you get a dress so quickly?"

She curtsied again. "Your husband, ma'am. There is a ladies clothing boutique near the inn, and Mr. Armstrong chose this for you himself."

He went out again? In the storm? To a *ladies clothing establishment?* "Thank you," she said, feeling a little breathless.

She took the box and placed it on the bed to open it. The midnight blue taffeta dress she pulled out was surprisingly well-made for a non-tailored garment, with drapings of silk and trimmings of lace. She wondered if it had been the most expensive dress in the shop. While it was not close in quality to what Anna was used to, it was likely the best they had and Pen had acquired it for her. His thoughtfulness moved her.

She stood in front of the fire and sighed again.

She had behaved very badly toward him earlier and endangered herself in the process. But her actions had not been without reason. His behavior had not been without fault. Plus, facing rejection from the man one had fallen in love with often led to irrational behavior.

As much as it pained her, she was making peace with her situation in regards Pen—or at least she was trying to. She could not force him to feel things he did not want to feel. Anna had not anticipated falling in love with the man. The extraordinary effect he had on her could not be ignored, but the fact had remained that he was not part of her plans for the future.

It was almost funny. Here she was pining for a man she could never have while her best friend was married to one who had potentially abducted her. Though she had to consider the other possibility, too. Libby *could* love Sir Anthony. He had presented himself well enough to create that option. If that were the case, it was just very unfortunate that Libby had never told Anna about him.

These thoughts were like a blade to her heart, and they thrust deep and twisted.

She and Libby shared everything. It was why their friendship was so strong.

The maid cleared her throat and brought Anna out of her reverie.

"Oh, yes. Help me out of this dress, please." She walked to the mirror in the corner of the room. Her dress had a row of tiny velvet-covered buttons, at least two dozen.

"What is your name?" Anna asked as the girl began unfastening the buttons. She wanted to distract herself with conversation, however small.

"I am Marguerite, ma'am," the girl replied timidly. She reminded Anna a little of Eva.

Eva had been very shy when she'd started working for Anna's family, but had soon broken free of that timidity with Anna's encouragement. Now she brought her the latest gossip…including the bit that had exposed Van Daal.

Anna made a mental note to reward Eva when she returned home.

"Are you French?" she asked the girl. Keeping her mind on the present was proving to be quite the endeavor.

"Yes. My *maman*, bless her soul, moved here with me fourteen years ago." Marguerite was visibly more comfortable now.

Anna gave her a small smile. "I am originally from England, but I have lived in Boston almost all my life."

"Oh, I hear Boston is a charming city." The girl's emerald green eyes sparkled.

Charming was not the word Anna would use for Boston. Fecund was more appropriate. Boston had a way of pulling one into it's depths. It brought together people from different parts of the world.

Likely, this young girl would not understand. "It is charming," was all she said, in the end.

"I dream of going there someday."

Dreams... Anna wondered if she would ever attain any of *her* dreams. They seemed very far away right now.

When all the buttons were undone and she was freed from the wet clothing, Marguerite bent and collected Anna's muddied boots and then laid the dress over her arm.

"I will have these dried for you, ma'am. Will you be needing anything else at this time?"

"That is all for now, Marguerite."

The girl curtsied again and left, and Anna was once again alone with her thoughts. She raised her eyes to her reflection, unsure what to make of the thin woman in her undergarments looking back. She did not recognize the defeat in those blue eyes, the tear tracks staining her cheeks, or the sadness pulling down the corners of her mouth. This was not her.

It couldn't be!

No, she was Lady Anna Trevallyn, a strong fearless woman with the vivacity of ancient goddesses. When she fell, she rose back up and continued with her head held high and her chin proud. Always. She was a duchess in her own right!

And she was not a sniveler. Her hands went up to wipe the tear marks from her face, then behind her head to remove the pins from her hair.

She used the water in the basin to splash her face and clean herself, and then rolled her hair back into that convenient bun at her nape. The fastenings of her new dress were at the front, so she did not require any help re-dressing. She was back in her chair beside the fire warming herself when Marguerite returned with her boots, cleaned and polished. As she was putting them on, another knock sounded and she asked Marguerite to answer the door.

"It is your husband, ma'am," the girl said, her face vermilion.

Anna's heart thumped. It took her a moment to remember that she was supposed to be Penforth's wife.

"He is ready to take you down to dinner."

"I will join him shortly."

Marguerite informed him, curtsied respectfully,

and closed the door before covering her flushed cheeks with her hands. Pen had that effect on women. Apparently they all turned pink and simple-minded in his presence.

"That will be all, Marguerite."

With that, Anna opened the door and stepped out to meet her supposed "husband".

CHAPTER THIRTEEN

It was as if his mind had been indoctrinated for years to react this way whenever he saw her. His breathing would slow and his eyes would roam over her figure as he allowed himself to appreciate her radiance, before he gained control of himself and shut everything down once again. Tonight was different, however. He was like a young man, without a grip on his feelings.

"Good evening, Pen," she greeted as she stepped into the hallway.

The blue dress he'd chosen for her looked lovely. It was not the dress a woman of her rank should wear, but she imbued it with elegance and grace.

He put forth all effort to show only equanimity, but he was not sure he succeeded. It was not until he had picked up her hand and raised it to his lips that he realized he had been staring at her like a fool.

"Good evening, Anna," he murmured after softly kissing her knuckles.

She allowed him to lead her downstairs to the private dining room he'd reserved. He disliked public places, but more than that, the privacy would enable them to talk freely. They skirted the public dining area but despite that, all heads turned to look at them as they passed through. He suspected their gazes were more on Anna and he automatically pulled her close in a possessive manner.

He thought maybe she released a snort, but at least she didn't pull away. Once in the private room, he led her to the table set for their dinner and pulled out a chair. She deserved a proper meal since she likely had not had one for a while. The inn did not have the modern gas lighting such as that in his own or Anna's residences, but the candles in their sconces created a cozy and intimate atmosphere.

While Pen took his seat, Anna uncovered the dishes and let out a small sound of pleasure. Creamy vegetable soup, roast beef with potatoes, and an apple pie, were laid out on the table and obviously met with her approval.

She smiled at the sight of the food and he could not help but smile too.

"I am starving," she declared, picking up her spoon and dipping it into the soup.

So was he. Wordlessly, they began to eat.

Only after they'd finished the first course and started on their second, did either of them speak again. "What are we going to do now?" Anna asked.

"We need to interrogate as many other people in the area as we can," he replied.

"Interrogate?"

"Well, question them. Not the innkeeper, though. The man seems dubious. I suggest we keep him in the dark as much as possible. I also think we need to go back to that chapel. I want to poke around some more."

She nodded, chewing thoughtfully. "There was something not right about that chapel," she agreed. "It felt…wrong."

Her comment reminded him of a lapse. "How do *you* feel?" He ought to have asked that as soon as he saw her.

"I feel much better, thank you. The headache is almost gone." She avoided his gaze as she answered.

"You're hurt more than you're letting on, aren't you?"

She took her time, raising another morsel to her mouth, and he waited patiently. When she swallowed, she immediately filled her mouth again with more food. The clever minx thought she could escape his question.

"Anna."

She put down her cutlery, took a small sip of wine, and dabbed at her mouth with a napkin before meeting his gaze.

"I am not going home before we find Libby," she said. "It doesn't matter how hurt I am—"

"It does to me," he cut her off.

"You're not sending me back. This is not about me. It's about Libby who is out there somewhere, most likely in some kind of trouble. Even if she's perfectly fine, we still need to find her and confirm that," she insisted.

"I understand, Anna, and we will find her," he said gently. "I am not going to send you back. I only need you to be honest with me at all times because I want you safe and healthy."

She pursed her lips as if in thought, then said at last, "Honesty. Very well. I have a few bumps and bruises, but nothing that won't heal quickly."

His immediate reaction to that was a strong need to send her packing, but he clamped his mouth shut. She had done him the honor of being truthful, after all. Eventually, he sighed. "Thank you for being honest. Now, back to Libby. I don't believe she would have married Sir Anthony willingly, no matter what anyone says. It is out of character for her to do such a thing."

She perked up. "I completely agree."

"My father ensured that both my sisters would never want for anything. He secured funds in a trust for both of them. Over the years, I've added significantly to the amount. Upon marriage, Libby will gain control of those funds. Or at least, her husband will."

Something began to simmer in her eyes. "I see. So, Sir Anthony likely thinks he can get his hands on the funds now that they are wed."

"He may if he remains married to her, however, I cannot see how it is possible that he knows about the trust at all."

Anna sniffed. "*I* don't understand why a woman would need to be married before she is given access to what is rightfully *hers*. Nor do I understand why her husband should be given access to *Libby's* funds upon marriage. *You* get to access and do whatever you please with *your* money so why can't it be the same for Libby or Mary? This wouldn't be happening if she had full control of her own funds."

"It's the law, Anna."

"Well, it's not fair."

He had to agree with her there. "You are right."

"When you made these laws, it was not to protect women's interests, but to satisfy your misogynistic cravings."

Her words unaccountably hurt. "I didn't make the laws."

"But you could have changed the terms, and given her access once she came of age. Look what my father did for me. He made me a duchess, despite most of society believing he'd gone mad. He stuck to what he believed was right—equality—and my life is so much the better for it. I have *choices*. Unlike Libby and Mary."

"Well, I…" He had no sensible response to that. Now that he was in charge of his family, it was indeed within his capacity to change things. He just hadn't thought about it. Not until the woman seated opposite him forced him to see the inequity. He began to gain a glimmer of understanding about what Anna and women like her were fighting for. It was just a tragedy that it had taken his sister becoming a possible victim of abduction and fraud for him to realize it.

"I will make amends," he said. Her eyes widened as if in shock and he was lost as to why, but he continued, nevertheless. "Once we return to Boston, I will see Libby gets her funds. And Mary, too, once she is of age."

"I must admit, I am quite surprised," she said.

He almost laughed. "You think me so unyielding and indifferent?"

She looked away. "You have not exactly given me cause to think otherwise. Until now."

A warm feeling filled him at the thought of receiving her approval. He reached across the table and took one of her hands. When it came to Anna, he had been a coward, and this time, he was not going to allow his fears to get in the way. He was going to let her know how he felt.

"I don't care for social gatherings," he began.

She gave him a confused frown. "What does that have to do with anything?"

"Since my return to Boston, every ball, every event, every soirée you have hosted, I have attended. The ones to which I was directly invited and the ones only my mother and Libby were supposed to attend. I have not missed a single one."

She still looked confused, but she was allowing him to talk. He needed her to understand what he was saying.

"I don't care for social gatherings," he repeated, "but I attended yours so I could see *you*."

Anna's shoulders slumped and her eyes misted. "Why?" she whispered.

"Because I couldn't stay away, Anna. I have been in denial of my feelings, but I made use of every opportunity to see you." Pen stared directly into her eyes. He wanted her to really understand what he'd hidden for so long. "I told myself many lies, about keeping an eye on my sister, or the fact that your foolish notions of utopia simply *entertained* me."

"They are not foolish notions," she said softly.

"I know that now."

She drew a long breath. "What are you trying to say, Pen?"

His free hand found her other hand and clasped it. His next words were the hardest because they exposed him the most. "You mean a lot to me. You were right, I don't care for much in this harsh world, but I do care about you. And I want to share your life if you will have me."

"Oh, Pen." Her voice was so low he had to strain to hear. "All this while, I thought you couldn't stand me."

A little smile curved his mouth. "Far from it. I

pushed you away because I was afraid of the strength of my feelings. I do not wish to lose you."

She burst out laughing. "You are the most impossible man I've ever met."

"*Have* I lost you?" His cheeks had heated most uncomfortably, but the question had to be asked.

"Of course not."

At her vehement declaration he jumped up and sped around the table to where she sat. He pulled her to her feet and circled his arms about her waist, pulling her close. The light from the candle danced in her eyes as she gazed up at him, and her lips parted. What he could only describe as a lovely feeling of rightness began to unfurl in his chest, sending warmth and light to the coldest and darkest corners of his being.

Inch by inch, his mouth neared hers. He drew out the moment to savor the anticipation. When their lips finally touched, it was sweetness and sensuality harmoniously mixed. Her arms drifted up to clutch at his shoulders. Now that he knew she felt the same, he was never going to let her go. He would do everything he could to make her happy.

His hands cradled her face and he pulled away to look into her eyes. The level of emotion he saw almost knocked the wind out of him. Everything she'd concealed behind a mask of self-protection was laid bare for him to see.

Pen kissed her lips again and held her a bit longer.

"Shall we have dessert?" he asked at last, releasing her with much reluctance.

She grinned. "I don't say no to sweets."

He settled back in his seat and served up the apple pie, feeling happy for the first time in a long time.

Just as they finished, a rough male voice whispered nearby. "Did you see them?"

Pen carefully set down his fork and so did Anna as they both strained to hear more.

"Oh, I saw. I heard one of 'em is a Hoffman," another man's voice replied. "Do you know how much money them Hoffmans have?"

Pen stood as quietly as he could and looked about the room, searching for where the voices might be coming from. Following the sound, he discovered a second door partially hidden behind a tapestry and pressed his ear to it.

"If we do this right, we will be very rich."

Anna came up beside him and motioned for him to make room so she could listen in, too.

"How many ladies did you count? And who told

you one of them was a Hoffman?" This person seemed to be doubting the information.

"Five ladies were given fine rooms. I gave some of 'em the keys myself. Then Little Lily told me she heard the gentleman that accompanied them refer to himself as Alexander Hoffman and that his sister was one of the five."

Anna tapped his arm and mouthed, "I know Rowena Hoffman."

He put his finger to his lips, warning her to stay quiet.

One of the men laughed. "Little Lily is going to help us win this game."

"To riches!" Glasses clinked and they laughed.

Pen and Anna remained by the door for a bit longer, listening for more, but it appeared that was all they would be getting. Pens suspected the men's revelation was linked somehow to Libby, and although they did not know what the men looked like, they now had a name. Little Lily.

"ANNA," PEN'S VOICE WAS QUIET. "WHO WAS THAT maid in your room earlier?"

"Do you mean Marguerite?"

He shrugged. "I guess so. Do you think you can question her?"

"Of course."

"Come." When he tucked her hand into the crook of his elbow it felt so right, and this time she held her head high as they walked out of the private dining room into the public area.

Like before, all eyes were on them as they crossed toward the entrance. Anna cast furtive glances around to see if she could find the men who'd been talking, but looks alone were not enough to determine anything, and there were many men in the room. It could be any one.

The innkeeper was behind the counter attending to guests as usual and when they caught his eyes, he grinned and bowed. They approached the desk.

"Good evening. How may I be of service to you?"

Anna took charge. "I gave the maid that was sent up to my chambers earlier my dress to clean and she is yet to return it." She left out the girl's name on purpose, so as not to seem too familiar with her. "Can you send her up to me?"

"Yes, my lady. Right away!"

Pen led Anna away and she waited until they were in her room before she spoke.

"If those men are right, then Rowena Hoffman is here, and potentially in some kind of danger."

"There does appears to be something big afoot," he mused.

"Should we warn them? You can seek out Alexander—"

"No, not yet. We should allow things to play out a little, and follow the trail. It could lead us to Libby."

"What if someone gets hurt?"

His eyes were like black steel when he said, "I won't let it come to that."

A knock sounded just then and Anna crossed the room to open the door.

"You asked for me, ma'am?" Marguerite curtsied. Anna's dress was in her arms.

"Yes, come in." Anna stepped aside to allow her in before closing the door and turning the key in the lock.

Marguerite stopped short when she heard the sound of the key, and when she turned and saw Pen in the room, she began to tremble.

"It's all right," Anna said in a soft voice. "We are not going to harm you. I promise." She took the dress and set it down on the bed, then waved toward one of the chairs by the fireplace. "Please sit. Make yourself comfortable."

Marguerite shook her head. "I shouldn't."

"Why not?" Anna asked gently

The girl looked in Pen's direction then back at Anna, her large eyes showing fear.

"Don't worry about him. Pretend he is not here."

Pen raised an affronted brow at Anna, which she ignored.

"I might get in trouble if I sit," Marguerite said in a shaky voice.

"It's just us here."

"Mr. Baker once saw me sitting on the fine furniture and I got lashed for it."

"Who is Mr. Baker?"

"The innkeeper."

The thought of Marguerite being struck by that man made Anna feel sick. She moved close to the young girl. "Does he strike you often?"

She nodded. "When I do something wrong. Even when I don't. The only maid he does not whip is Little Lily. He likes that one."

Anna's gaze met Pen's and he gave her a nod of encouragement. Marguerite knew quite a bit from the sound of it, and her dislike of Mr. Baker could work to their advantage. She placed her hands on Marguerite's shoulders and gently urged her to sit. Then she sat opposite.

"Tell me about your work with Mr. Baker."

She looked unsure.

"We will protect you. I give you my word," Pen said and Anna nodded in concurrence.

"Ten years ago, my *maman* started working for him to repay her debt to him. Seven years ago, she died of the fever, and he made me continue her work. He has never paid me. He just beats me and calls me names." She sniffled. "My memory is not very good, but I think he beat my mother too."

The wretched innkeeper had been abusing the poor girl for years.

Anna offered her a handkerchief from her purse, and Marguerite accepted it gratefully. "You said he liked Little Lily and didn't hurt her."

With a nod of her head, she continued. "He offers her to some of the guests and she brings him the money. It is why he likes her. But there is something else, ma'am. Lily likes to drink, you see, and when she drinks, she talks. They have a new business now. They are planning to make money off proper ladies like you. They will kidnap them and ask their families for ransom or force them to marry one of the men so they can get their hands on their fortunes. The *Blue Chapel* arranges such weddings all the time."

Anna's heart started beating very fast at the

thought of Libby caught up in such an ordeal. She cast a quick glance at Pen, whose mouth was a tight slash of contained emotion.

"Do you know anyone by the name of Sir Anthony Hart?" Anna asked.

"No, ma'am, I don't."

She then showed off the portrait of Libby, and although Marguerite did not recognize her, Anna knew there was simply too much about this to be unconnected to Libby's plight.

"I overheard some of the men Mr. Baker works with talking about some ladies that arrived today," Marguerite supplied.

They were most likely the same men Anna and Pen had overheard downstairs.

"Do you know what they look like?"

"Yes. I can tell you which room they are staying in, and their names." At Anna's nod, she gave the names: Vincent Day and William Singer.

William Singer was the man who hired Van Daal to watch Libby. He knew where Libby was and he'd been at the wedding ceremony. This was it! This was their link.

"Do you want to get out of here, Marguerite? I mean, for good?"

"Yes! I have dreamed of it."

"We need your help, and in return, we will take

you back to Boston with us. You can have a place in my residence if you wish."

Her eyes filled with tears. "You would do that, ma'am?"

"Yes. It's a promise." She stood and Pen shifted close. "Now, show us where these men are."

CHAPTER FOURTEEN

Marguerite took them to another part of the inn and knocked on the door of the room William Singer and Vincent Day were staying in, announcing, "Housekeeping!"

No one came to the door.

She knocked several times and was met with silence. Then she tried opening the door and found it locked.

"They might still be down at the bar," she offered.

"I'll go down and see if I can find them there," Pen said. "Anna, I need you to go back to your room and stay there until I return."

"Shouldn't we check in here first?" She gestured at the locked door.

He shook his head. "They could return at any moment. I don't want to risk it."

"All right." She would have liked to convince him otherwise, but his posture brokered no argument.

Marguerite accompanied Pen to help identify the hooligans while Anna made a show of going back to her room. She went up a level and crossed the hall toward her door. Then waited a minute or two before turning around and going back down to that room.

She was nervous. She'd never broken into a room before and didn't know what would happen if she were caught. Reminding herself that she was doing this for Libby gave her the resolve she needed. With a glance around to confirm that no one was coming, she pulled two pins out of her hair and inserted them into the keyhole. After what felt like forever, the lock gave and she quickly stepped inside.

An intense musty smell mixed with something she couldn't place assaulted her nose. The room was untidy with clothes strewn about, a half-eaten meat pie and an empty bottle of wine on a desk by the window. The bed was unmade. She surmised that the stink she'd been unable to place initially was emanating from the rotting meat pie on the desk.

Did the maids not clean this room?

There were candles already lit in sconces on the wall, which supplied enough light for a search. Placing her hands on her hips, she looked about, not sure where to begin. She did not know what exactly she should be looking for.

A drawer by the bed seemed like a good place to start. She opened it and began rummaging through, thankful she was wearing gloves. Nothing in this room seemed clean. She found a piece of folded paper, dirty from handling, and unfolded it. In rough, almost illegible writing was a list of names; she recognized two from the list and as her eyes moved down, she caught the name Elizabeth Armstrong-Leeds. Libby! The entry was struck out with a pencil. Her blood froze in her veins as she began to fear the worst.

Shoving the paper into her dress pocket, she searched more. Maybe she might find something else to indicate where Libby was being kept.

The sound of footsteps met her ears and she stilled, listening for where the person was heading. She pushed the drawer shut before crouching. The footsteps stopped in front of the door and before she had any time to reconsider her actions, she flattened herself onto the floor and slithered beneath the bed.

Her heartbeat drummed loudly in her ears and she sent up a silent prayer for her own safety. The door opened and booted feet entered. Anna held her breath as the person walked about the room, grumbling to themselves. "First he leaves the door open with the lights on and now all the wine is gone."

If he was blaming someone else for the door being open then he must not suspect her presence. *Thank goodness.*

She heard a couple of unidentifiable thunks, and carefully turned her head. Boots, black and thick with mud, were on the floor near her face. She quickly shut her eyes and sucked in her breath, while her heart picked up the pace.

The bed above her creaked when it received his weight and she silently let out the breath she was holding. For a moment, she'd thought that he'd found her. He stretched on the bed. It didn't take long before she heard the rough sound of a snore.

Dear God! She was trapped.

The bar had emptied when Pen and Marguerite arrived and he pulled out his pocket watch to check the time. It was not so late; just past nine o'clock. Three men sat at the bar drinking while two more were playing cards at a table in the corner.

"Do you see them?" he asked Marguerite in a low voice.

"The three at the bar," she whispered. "The bald one on the left is William Singer."

He clenched his jaw to control his rising choler. "I'll handle it from here. Go back to your room and wait for my wife and me. We'll find you when we can."

Now that the girl had assisted them, he did not trust she would be safe. He was glad Anna had offered to bring her back with them to Boston.

There was an empty stool beside the man supposed to be William Singer and Pen made himself comfortable on it. "Whiskey," he said to the barmaid. She gave him a flirtatious smile before pouring the drink.

"Whiskey is not the only thing we serve here, sir," she said, giving him a suggestive grin.

Ah, this would likely be Little Lily.

Pen pretended to take a sip of his drink and then turned to William Singer. "Arnold, is that you?" He clapped the man on the back.

Singer started and gave him a look more drunken than surprised.

"Huh?"

"It's me, Ashford. Don't you remember me?"

"No..." the man muttered.

Pen shrugged casually. "Oh, I don't blame you. It was a long time ago." Then he clapped the man on the back again. "Good to see you, old pal." To the barmaid, he said aloud, "Serve my friend another round. In fact, I am buying for everyone in this room!"

Singer and his fellow thugs began to cheer. "I still don't remember you, but I like you," he slurred, returning Pen's clap on his back.

Since the men were not paying for their ale, they drank greedily and it did not take long for one of them to slump over the table, drooling and mumbling nonsense. When no one was looking, Pen poured his whiskey into Singer's ale and asked the barmaid for more.

"So tell me, Arnold. What are you doing in this place?"

Singer stretched his lips and cheeks to form a stupid smile, baring crooked teeth. "Singer... Singer...is me."

"Oh!" Pen feigned innocence then laughed out loud. "I must be truly mistaken." He waved his hand about like he was drunk. "So what are you doing here, my friend?"

"Business…" He gulped down the rest of his spiked ale and pushed the mug toward the barmaid to refill. "Very…*profitable* business." He stumbled over the word profitable, clearly well intoxicated.

"What sort of business? I am looking to make some money myself. Maybe we could work together, eh?"

"Ahhhh…good idea…" He leaned very close, inconveniencing Pen with his bad breath. "There are some ladies we want to *collect.*" He stressed *collect* as if it were code for something, "And then ask their families for ransom. It was my idea…we…we… could force the ladies to marry us, but I reasoned ransom will be better. Hmm?"

"Yes, my friend."

"So, a couple of days ago…I…err…was hired to collect a lady in Boston. The man who hired me married her, but she is refusing to give him the money he wants. Now he wants…me—" he pointed at his chest, "—to get rid of her."

At the moment of that revelation, Pen understood what true fear really was.

ONCE SHE WAS SURE THE MAN ABOVE HER WAS soundly sleeping, Anna shifted from under the bed, careful not to make a sound. He had been snoring for a while now. On her hands and knees, she began to crawl in the direction of the door, dodging the dirty clothes in her path.

The bed creaked as he turned and she quickly flattened herself on the floor. Like a cold claw around her throat, uncertainty choked her. He could wake up and find her. She waited for her nerves to calm and to also give him time to settle back into sleep. Once he was snoring again, she continued her perilous crawl to the door.

When she reached the door, she straightened but remained on her knees. Standing and risking her shoes making any sound against the wooden floor was not an option. Her hand shook as she reached for the door handle. She turned it and it made a small sound.

"Hmmm?"

Her head snapped in the direction of the bed, eyes wide, throat dry, and heart thumping. He was still asleep, thankfully. With her gaze trained on him, she pulled the door and shuffled out of the room, then shut it behind her with an inevitable click. Anna jumped to her feet and began to run.

When she realized no one was following her, she slowed down and leaned against the wall to catch her breath. Perhaps Pen was right and luck did exist, after all.

Her breathing slowed and she regained some of her composure. She had two options: either return to her room where Pen expected she'd be, or go downstairs and try to find him. She straightened her skirts, and set off down the stairs.

She made for the bar and found him sitting and drinking with a rough-looking group of men. The room was empty save for Pen and his three companions, a barmaid behind the counter, and a gentleman sitting at a corner table gathering cards. He looked like he was readying to leave. She waited by the door, watching Pen talk to the drunk man beside him; she could hardly make out his words.

"Excuse me."

Her head snapped up to find the gentleman who had been gathering cards in front of her. She stared at him confusedly.

"May I pass, please?"

It registered that she was blocking the doorway. "Oh, pardon me." She stepped into the room and he walked past her. She found a table not far from Pen and sat. It would make no sense if she walked up to them and interrupted. It looked as though he was getting good information from the drunk man.

Suddenly, Pen grabbed the man's shirt front.

"Where is she?"

"Get yer hands off me," the drunk man slurred, trying to slap Pen's hand away.

"Where is she!" Pen shook him.

The man freed himself from Pen's grasp and tried to punch him but missed. He swung again and connected with Pen's jaw. Anna winced. It took but a fraction of a moment for Pen to recover and he pulled his arm back and let fly, knocking the man to the ground. There he straddled him.

"Where is she?"

The man did not answer. He only struggled to get Pen off him. The thug on the second stool chose that moment to emerge from his stupor and came to his companion's rescue. He caught Pen from behind, drunkenly trying to pull him up. There was no way Anna could sit and watch so she jumped in, climbing onto the back of the man holding Pen and pulling at his hair.

The scuffle occupied everyone and they failed to notice the third man who had been slumped on the counter stagger to his feet and begin gathering up a chair.

Anna was no match for the man she had attacked; he was large and strong. He threw her off without much effort. She fell to the floor and that was when she noticed the man with the chair. His progress was slow, but his gaze was fixed on Pen's head. She glanced wildly around, noticing a glass jug on one of the tables. She moved with a speed she could never have believed herself capable of before today. Just as the man raised the chair, the jug connected with the back of his head, sending him crashing to the floor, chair and all.

The noise distracted the others and Pen struggled out from underneath the pile of bodies and drew a revolver. The man Anna had clouted was out cold. The second man raised his arms in a gesture of surrender and slowly backed away toward the door, When he was close enough to the exit, he took to his heels, leaving behind Anna, Pen, and the man he'd originally been questioning.

Pointing the revolver at the man's head, Pen told him to stand up. If someone walked into this room now, they would all have some explaining to do.

"Pen," she said, "we need to leave."

He looked about before gesturing toward a door behind the counter. "There is a room back there."

It was then that Anna realized the barmaid was nowhere to be found. It was no surprise, however. If Anna had been in her position, she would have run away, too. With the gun pointed at his back, the man was directed behind the counter into what proved to be a large storeroom. Pen forced the man to sit on the lone chair, and Anna closed the door to keep out prying eyes.

"Here." Pen handed Anna the revolver while he bound the prisoner's hands behind the chair with a handy length of rope from one of the shelves.

Pen looked as if he'd been pushed to his limit. He was clearly teetering on the edge. It distressed her to see him this way.

He took back the gun and the interrogation recommenced. "Where is Lady Elizabeth Armstrong-Leeds?"

"I don't know," the man whimpered. One of his injured eyes had closed over and was beginning to turn purple.

"Let me give you your options, Singer..."

Anna's mouth opened. *This* was William Singer? The man for whom Van Daal had betrayed her family. The man at Libby's fake wedding. Oh, this scoundrel deserved whatever was coming to him!

"...you can tell us the truth or you can keep it to yourself. It doesn't matter what you choose, you are not leaving this room a free man. If you don't tell us, however, the police will get it out of you one way or the other."

The room fell silent as they waited for a

response. He must have realized his freedom was finally over because eventually, he began to speak, albeit in a sullen tone.

"Anthony Hart asked me to kill her because she will not cooperate. If she dies, he can present marriage papers and claim her fortune."

A shiver of horror ran through her.

So *that* was why Libby's name had been struck through.

"The names on the paper you kept hidden in a drawer in your room upstairs. Are they all people you've been hired to kill?" Anna asked. Pen shot her a confused look, which she returned with a look that said *not now*.

"No, she is the only one to be killed. The rest are supposed to be kept captive."

At that moment they heard a tiny whimper. There was someone else in the room. Someone hiding. Pen reached into his coat and pulled out a second gun. *What on earth*? She thought, with not a small measure of astonishment, that he'd certainly come prepared for battle. She took the second gun, a Colt, from him, and confidently cocked the hammer.

It was no secret around town that she was good with firearms and she'd won many a challenge against gentlemen trying to prove their superiority.

Cautiously, she searched corners and any conceivable hiding place until she reached a stack of wooden crates near the back of the room. Behind it, she found the barmaid.

She began to lower the Colt, until the girl crawled out and Pen barked, "That's Little Lily."

Anna's arm rose straight back up. "Get over there near Singer," she ordered. The girl crawled across the floor, but Anna refused to feel sorry for her. She was in on the plan to capture the ladies and that made her a criminal, too.

She handed Pen back the gun and found another length of rope. This one she used to bind Lily's arms and legs.

Once she had been secured, Pen handed her back the gun, and they returned their attention to William Singer.

"Where are you keeping her?"

"The *Blue Chapel*," Singer responded, his head bowed in resignation. "There is a crypt beneath."

Anna's heart began to pound so hard she could barely hear any more. There was only one thought in her head now and it was a prayer. A prayer for Libby to be all right. A prayer for her friend to hold on just a little bit longer.

We're coming, Libby. Please be alive.

CHAPTER FIFTEEN

Rushing out of the inn with Anna's hand in his was a blur. They raced across the road, dodging carriage traffic, to reach the chapel. The storm that had earlier ravaged the town had retreated, but bone-chilling drizzle and a thick fog were left behind as sentry; to obstruct the weary traveler's vision and beat down their resolve with chilling precision.

Yes, nature was kind that way.

But Penforth and Anna together, were formidable opponents. They pushed through the shrouding fog and darkness to reach Elizabeth.

The minister obviously didn't expect them back, and he answered the door without checking first to see who was on the other side. When Mr. Anders saw them, he tried to close the heavy doors but Pen wedged himself through the gap and caught the man by the collar. "Oh, no you don't," he commanded.

The *Blue Chapel's* days of collecting bribes, arranging unfavorable weddings and assisting in kidnappings, were over.

"This is a holy place," the minister blustered. "You cannot come in here and threaten a man of God." Pen pushed him onto one of the pew benches.

"A man of God who holds a woman prisoner in his church," Pen spat. He tried to resist pointing the gun at him. No matter what this place had been turned into, it was still hallowed ground and he respected that.

There were no ropes in sight, so Pen took his handkerchief and bound it with two of Anna's. It wasn't ideal but was long enough to bind the man's hands in front of him. Pen had him slide his arms through the gap at the back of the pew first, so that he couldn't run away once bound.

"We've been told Elizabeth Armstrong-Leeds is here. Tell us where to find the crypt."

Mr. Anders remained tight-lipped. He turned his face to the side like a petulant child.

"Fine. If she is in this building, we will find her.

But mark my words, you will not be leaving this place a free man."

They found a door on the right side by the transept, opened it, and ran down a dark narrow hallway to a set of steps leading downward. Were these the crypts Singer had told them about? Only one way to find out.

At the base of the stairs, a wooden arched door stood between them and the other side. It had no handle, only a keyhole.

"The key must be with Mr. Anders," Anna suggested.

"Stay here. I'll get the key from him."

She shook her head. "I don't want to waste any more time. Libby might be on the other side of this. I can open it."

Before he could say anything, she reached into her hair and retrieved a hairpin. Pen watched in astonishment as she maneuvered the pin and unlocked the door with the precision of a thief. As a matter of fact, not every thief was in possession of such a skill.

"Perhaps I should not ask where you learned how to do that," he said.

She grinned with a level of ferocity that caused his heart to beat faster. "I played with my father's clocks instead of learning to sew and paint, so they would lock the clocks away or place them in high places where I couldn't reach. One of our serving girls taught me to do this and with a lot of practice, I learned to open different kinds of locks."

Just then, the lock gave way and she pushed open the door. Pen shook his head. She was full of surprises. From saving his life—which he needed to thank her for later—to opening locks as easily as a jewel thief. Anna was a brilliant woman. He wished he'd had the courage to own his feelings a lot earlier.

The chamber was dark, dank, and made him very uncomfortable. The dead obviously rested here. It was no place to hold a live person.

He blinked several times to allow his eyes to adjust to the darkness and was able to make out the shadow of a candlestick on a small side table near the door. Anna was already there and she had found a match because the place suddenly brightened.

Pen took the candle holder from her after she'd lit several candles in their sconces, and took her hand in his. Slowly, they made their way through the chamber, and near the end, saw the form of a person slumped in a chair.

"Oh, my God, Libby?" Anna gasped and hurried toward the figure.

It *was* his sister. And she was alive. He almost sank to his knees with relief when the figure lifted her head and stared at them. He set the candlestick on the floor and went to her. Anna was already loosening the ropes binding his sister's hands, so he got to work on her ankles.

"Took you long enough," Libby rasped. She was clearly trying for bravado, but he could hear the quiver of relief in her words. "Do you know how dark and lonely this place is?"

She was going to be all right. The spirit in her had not been doused by her captivity. But her face was bruised and the corner of her lip was crusted with dried blood.

Pen's jaw clenched. Every person involved in hurting his sister would pay. He would not rest until they were found and brought to justice.

"If you only knew what we went through to find you," Anna said.

"I knew you would come," Libby whispered. "I couldn't think of anything else."

Anna wrapped Libby into her embrace once she was freed. "I am so sorry, Libby. We took far too long to find you."

His sister held on to Anna tightly. "No, Anna. *I* am sorry. This is all my fault. I was careless and stupid."

"Let's not talk about it now." Anna smoothed a lock of Libby's dirty hair off her cheek, and Pen was struck by her capacity for care. "Let's get you out of here. Are you able to stand?"

She nodded and Anna helped her to her feet. That was when Libby finally acknowledged Pen. "Hello, brother," she said. "I didn't mean to ignore you. Anna was smothering me."

Anna let out an amused chuckle as he folded Libby into his arms. "You're safe now, sister. Let's get you out of here."

Libby suddenly stiffened in his arms. "Mary," she exclaimed. "How is Mary?"

"She is fine and at home waiting for your return. As is Mother."

She sighed with relief. "I was so worried about her."

The backs of his eyes stung and he blinked hard. "You don't have to worry about anything anymore," he assured her. "Let's go home."

"Not so fast!" The new voice behind them was sharp and accusatory. He turned to find Mr. Anders pointing a gun at them. With Pen's own handkerchief still dangling from one of the man's wrists. *Oh, for the love of God!*

What had he been thinking, failing to bind the minister's hands securely enough? Pen began to reach for his own gun, going against his earlier decision to respect hallowed ground.

"Oh, no you don't!" Mr. Anders warned. "Move again and I will shoot." His gun was pointed directly at Libby.

"What do you want?" Pen asked him.

"Money, of course. And my freedom."

"Always money," Anna rolled her eyes.

Pen begged her with his eyes to be careful. At least, he hoped she could read that message in his quick frown.

"And freedom?" she continued. "If that means so much to you, why did you hold a woman captive?"

"I was paid."

"Do you not have a conscience?"

"You say that because you have money. You were born to privilege. You don't know what it feels like to worry about your family starving."

Anna scoffed. "Now, that is utter humbug. You get paid by the church and you get paid well, too." The man was an idiot if he thought he could fool Anna into believing his nonsense. Pen figured she probably knew more about the wage system than he did.

The minister's attention was fully on Anna now. This gave Pen the opportunity to quickly release his revolver and fire. The shot grazed the other man's hand and catapulted the minister's gun away, and he sank to the ground with a scream. "You shot me! You shot me!"

Anna raced over and collected up the gun. Libby finally moved, gathering her heavy dress in her hands and walking up to the prone minister. She landed a kick in the middle of his back. "My brother showed you mercy!" Her boot connected again. "Your knuckles are grazed, no worse than a fist fight. I would have truly shot you, right between the eyes!" She let out a string of expletives that would make a sailor gape.

Pen interceded and pulled her to him. "It's all right, Libby. Let's go."

"No, it's not!" She pushed him away. "They've ruined my life! And probably Mary's, too." She broke down in tears, then, sobbing as if her heart would break.

He swept her up in his arms and made for the crypt exit. As he passed the minister, he saw Anna moving toward him and paused to see what she would do. She bent over Anders, drew her fisted hand back, and let fly. Pen winced at the force of the punch, even as his thoughts celebrated her action. He certainly would not want to be on the receiving end of a punch like that.

Anna did something strange with another hair clip and relocked the crypt behind them. She joined him as they left the chapel. "The shot hardly even grazed his hand," she said. "He'll be all right in there until we can get the police. Won't he?"

His heart swelled. Even in her anger against a nasty criminal, she was thinking about the wellbeing of others. "He'll be fine," he assured her. "I'll have my man James fetch the police at first light."

It was over now and Libby was safe, but some potentially lasting damage had been done. There was no denying that.

The fog was thicker than before and the streets were silent and deserted. Hours ago, the desertion in his heart would have mirrored that of these streets. But his heart in this moment was full. His sister was safe and the woman he loved reciprocated his feelings.

It didn't take long to rouse his man and organize for their carriage to be brought out front. He left James to arrange for the police first thing in the morning, and took it upon himself to drive the women to another establishment for rest. The *Lexington Inn* was not far from the *Five Castles* but a far more suitable abode in which to leave the women he cared for. There, he reserved a room for Anna and Libby, and another for himself.

He was loathe to leave the ladies by themselves, but there were matters that needed his attention: William Singer and his thugs needed to be detained until sunrise when the police would come and take them into custody.

He had requested a horse, and was preparing to return to the *Five Castles*, when a knock sounded on his door. When he opened it, Anna was standing there with two steaming mugs of chocolate.

"I thought you could use one of these."

Oh, Anna. How thoughtful.

She handed the mug to him and he took a large sip. The chocolate warmed him, but the gesture warmed him even more.

"Libby has had a bath and is resting. She is so very exhausted, poor thing."

Setting down his mug and then hers on a small table between the chairs by the fireplace, he took her dainty hands in his large ones. "How are *you*?" His fingers stroked her cheek tenderly. "You've hardly had any time to regain your bearing."

She closed her eyes and sighed. "I am glad this is over, Pen. I thought it would never end."

He had thought so, too. It had been like living a nightmare and at some point, he'd been convinced they would never see Libby alive again. He pulled Anna into his arms. She had been brave throughout. "Your courage is unlike any I've seen, Anna."

"Any woman, you mean?"

"No. Any person."

He felt her relax completely against him and he held her for a long moment before pulling away with great reluctance. "I have to leave now," he said, leaning forward to kiss her softly on the cheek.

"You've not finished your chocolate."

He chuckled, then raised the mug to his lips and drank it all in one long draft. "Happy?"

She nodded with a smile. "Be careful."

Pen pulled her close once again and pressed his lips to her forehead. "I will."

Libby was sitting up in bed hugging her knees to her chest when Anna returned to their room. She seemed lost, just staring into space. The sight was disturbing. Anna climbed onto the bed and sat beside her friend with her legs folded beneath her.

"Libby," she said, carefully touching her shoulder.

Her friend did not move. She continued to stare ahead unblinkingly.

Anna shook her slightly, and Libby finally released a sigh. "Anna, I caused this."

Her heart felt leaden at the words. She didn't want Libby blaming herself. How could this possibly have been her fault? She'd fallen victim to a diabolical scheme that had almost cost her her life. It was most definitely not her fault.

"You didn't cause this, Libby."

"What led you to find me?" She still had not looked at Anna.

"I went through your journal and found some of your letters."

Libby did turn to look at her then, her hazel eyes flat and hard. Anna suspected the loathing she read there was directed at herself rather than Anna. "Then you must know of Sir Anthony."

Anna gave a small nod.

"I had never met him prior to the incident. I first received his letter several months ago. He wrote that he saw me at one of the balls we'd attended but never got the chance to be introduced. I felt a sense of adventure in corresponding with a man I'd never met; it was intriguing." She paused and heaved a sigh of distress. Anna ran her palm up and down her friend's back in a soothing motion. That seemed to provide some comfort and eventually Libby continued. "He created an image of the perfect man; an advocate for equality, intellectual, well-traveled. We had very similar interests and I could not help but be enchanted by his words." She fell silent for a moment. "He wanted to meet with me and his last letter was an invitation to meet him in Cambridge. At first, I was incredibly happy and even penned down the location and date, but after some time and a bit more thinking, I felt something was wrong with his invitation. Why would a gentleman ask a lady to meet with him for the first time outside of town and in such secret circumstances? It didn't make sense. It was not proper. I responded, declining his invitation. I had thought to invite him to the house instead, but decided against that, too."

"Your response caused him to kidnap you," Anna whispered, horrified at what had been done.

"He thought he could lure me. Anna, what hurts the most is that I almost fell for his lies." Her voice was bitter with resentment.

She would need time to recover, and Anna hoped, for Libby's sake, that recovery would occur sooner rather than later. She normally had such a beautiful fiery spirit that seeing her like this broke Anna's heart.

"When I went up to change my dress, I saw a light in the garden from the window in my room. It seemed unusual because the light kept flashing continuously. I opened the window to see better, but in the end decided to go and check it out in person. Instead of going through the sunroom, I went toward the servants' entrance and that was where someone got me. They put a damp cloth to my nose and that's the last thing I remember until I woke up in a room and I was tied to a chair. He said that I would have to marry him and if I refused, he would hurt my family. Especially my little sister."

Anna rather thought it would be better if Libby stopped talking and rested, at least until the police interviewed her on the morrow. This recollection was clearly very difficult. "Libby, if talking about this is too hard—"

"No, Anna. I *want* to talk about it. It helps." She smiled a little then, and Anna was moved by the sight. Libby may have gone through a lot of suffering in the last couple of days but her spirit was still unbroken. For that, Anna was truly grateful. "It was a nightmare but it is over now. Right?"

"Yes," Anna confirmed. "Yes, it is."

Libby then stretched out and rested her head on Anna's shoulder. "He said he had men ready to take Mary if I did not cooperate. I believed him because of that incident with the maid in my room. You remember that, don't you?"

Anna had forgotten about it, until now. About four months ago, Libby caught a maid going through her things. Although nothing had been found missing, the girl, Maria, had refused to disclose what she had been looking for. Naturally, she had been dismissed with an investigation carried out that had yielded nothing.

"I do now. Do you recall that new footman, Van Daal? We found that he'd been paid to watch you the night of the soiree and for some time prior."

Libby raised her head to stare at Anna. "I knew something was not right with him. I felt his eyes on me throughout that evening." She shook her head. "You can't trust anyone these days."

"The driver who transported you here said that you were drunk."

"I sat tied up in that chair for a long time. Or, it felt like it, anyway. He gave me a drink. I had hoped for water but accepted the brandy thinking it would help with my nerves. He must have put something more in it because I don't really remember the journey to this place. Not a piece of it." She lowered her head back onto Anna's shoulder as she continued to relate the event. "I regained some of my sensibility in the chapel when he forced me to sign the marriage papers and the register. I did that for Mary."

"You thought you were saving her. You were trying to do the right thing. I would have done the same." She nudged her friend. "Libby, *I* would have done that if I thought *you* were in danger."

Her friend's eyes pooled and her chin quivered. "You came out here for me."

Anna wrapped her arms about Libby's shoulders. "Of course. And I would do it all over again."

They shared a quiet moment before Libby continued. "He gave me a document to sign. It would confirm that I married him willingly and of my own volition, which will immediately transfer all of my possessions and inheritance to him. I refused. He threatened me again, but I couldn't do it. Call it a delusion, but I felt that you and Pen were coming for me. It gave me the strength to resist. He put the damp cloth over my nose again and I blacked out. When I woke up, I was in the crypt, tied to a chair, yet again."

"I am glad you didn't sign the paper."

"So am I."

"Do you know where this scoundrel is?"

"He never came back. I haven't seen him since he put me in the crypt."

There was no indication that she knew a kill order had been placed on her head. That was a good thing and Anna preferred to keep it that way.

"I am sorry about your dress," Libby said after a long moment.

"A dress is nothing in the scheme of things," Anna answered in a light tone. "Besides, your brother already bought me another one."

Libby smiled and said slowly, "Did he now?"

Finally the calm of the night began to envelop them both and Anna lay down beside Libby. It would be good to get some rest at last. She was on the verge of sleep when she heard slow footsteps approaching their door. The hairs on the back of her neck instantly stood on end. Those weren't Pen's footsteps. His were sure and determined. These were slow and stalking.

Her body went rigid with fear, but she reached deep within herself to pull forth the will to not let fear take control.

Reaching under her pillow, she pulled out the Colt she'd placed there earlier and sat up, careful not to let the bed creak. Libby stared at Anna, the terror in her eyes a reflection of what Anna felt on the inside. She pressed a finger to her lips telling Libby to be quiet as she lowered her feet to the floor.

She padded across the room and stood about two feet from the door, her gun aimed directly at its center. Libby moved near, the fireplace poker raised in one hand. Whatever devil was on the other side of the door, they would face and defeat it, together.

The footsteps stopped right in front of the door. The air thickened with an amalgam of dread and resolute expectancy as the moment drew out. Every slow second that ticked by constricted Anna's nerves. Her hand tightened around the Colt and her thumb twitched in readiness.

Something white slipped into the room from underneath the door. A paper. And the footsteps began to retreat. Anna looked to an equally disoriented Libby and they waited until they could not hear anything before diving down to retrieve the paper. Libby got to it first, and Anna moved to her side to read what was on it. A single sentence written in ink: *I am not finished with you!*

CHAPTER SIXTEEN

In the search for his sister, Pen and Anna had inadvertently uncovered a crime that, though still in its infancy, greatly threatened the genteel ladies of Boston. These women were born into fortune, making them easy prey for the hard-hearted.

When Pen returned to the *Five Castles*, the first person he sought was James. He had some thought of gathering up their prisoners in the storeroom and moving them over to the church crypt, but when they returned to the bar, he was dismayed to discover the door open and their prisoners gone.

They went back to the front hall to find the innkeeper, but he was nowhere to be found. Instead, there was a new man standing behind the desk. His name plate said Julius Crispin.

"I am looking for Mr. Baker," Pen said to the man.

"He has retired for the night, sir. I am on duty now. Can I help you?"

Pen was not in the mood for politeness. "Get him for me."

Julius frowned. "But, sir—"

"I said. Get. Him. For. Me." A threat punctuated each of his words and the man scurried away.

After a long wait, he returned. "Mr. Baker is not in his chambers, sir."

Pen looked at him long and hard, subjecting him to intimidation to determine his veracity.

"I swear it. He was not there." The man cowered.

"Do you know William Singer or Vincent Day?"

Julius gulped and nodded, his brows creasing into a frown.

"Have you seen them?"

"I only commenced my shift two hours ago. I have not seen either of them in that time."

Pen inclined his head. "Why do you look nervous then?"

"Those men make me nervous. They are rough. I don't know why Mr. Baker is working with them."

This did not bode well. Either the innkeeper and the thugs had run away or they were out enacting their plan to collect other ladies on their list. Pen thought fast. "Where is Alexander Hoffman staying?"

The man blinked in confusion.

"Alexander Hoffman is a guest here. Which is his room?"

"Oh! Let me check." He consulted the register, his fingers moving down the names before settling on one. "There! He is on the fourth level. I can take you." He began to move around the counter.

Pen held up a hand to stop him. "I need you to stay here, and send word to me immediately if you see any of the men I am looking for."

"Right away, sir."

Pen headed for the stairs with James close behind. He paused at the foot of the stairs and turned.

"James, I need you to find someone for me," he said in a low voice. "A maid in this establishment by the name of Marguerite."

James nodded carefully and said, "I know her. I met her earlier."

"Good." He clapped him on the back. "Go find her. Once you do, take her to the *Lexington Inn*, to Lady Anna."

With that, he took the stairs two at a time to Alexander's room. He was acquainted with the man; even had one or two business dealings with him. There would be no need for introductions. He reached the room and began to knock. Not too loudly, but enough to wake the person sleeping within unless they slept like the dead.

Pen hoped he did not sleep like the dead: there were five ladies in his care.

The door opened and Hoffman stood before him barefoot and in his nightshirt, rubbing his eyes and squinting up at Pen. It took a moment for him to register who it was.

"Armstrong-Leeds? What the devil?" He was clearly surprised.

"We don't have much time, Hoffman. Where are the ladies in your care?"

He pointed toward a door down the hall. "Two are there." Then he pointed at the door next to it. "And three in there."

"I need you to not panic. I received word of an abduction plan and some of those ladies are the target."

"Good Lord!" Hoffman's eyes widened and he stepped out of the room into the hallway. "My sister…And Sophia…" Moving to the door on the left, he began to pound on the wood. It opened on the fourth knock and a red head poked out.

"Thank God, Rowena! Where is Martha?"

"She's here, sleeping."

Pen let out a relieved breath. Two had been accounted for.

"Good. Go back inside and lock this door. Don't open it for anyone. Don't open your windows either."

Alarm widened her eyes and she glanced nervously at Pen before asking, "Is something wrong?"

"Nothing. Only that this place is not very safe, especially for young ladies."

Her worried look quickly turned into a glare. "Then why did you bring us here?"

"Rowena, dear, I am sure you remember the storm that drove us inside," Hoffman replied, sounding irritated.

"It is over now. We can leave."

A sigh of frustration escaped. "It is past three in the morning," Hoffman said through clenched teeth. "Now do as I say. Go back in and lock your door."

She complied without further dissent just as the other door opened. A dark-haired woman, about Anna's age, stepped out.

"Alex, what's going on?" she asked.

Hoffman rushed to her and took her in his arms. "Sophia…"

A large stone on her left hand glittered in the hall lamps and Pen determined her to be Hoffman's fiancée.

"This place is not very safe and I wanted to make sure you are all right," he said, pulling away.

She smiled and reassured him. "I am fine."

"Your sisters?"

"Still sleeping soundly."

He kissed her forehead then. "Go back in and lock the door. Do not open it to anyone except me, or Rowena. Do you hear me?"

The woman nodded, suddenly wide-eyed.

"We will leave as soon as the sun is up. Now go, and don't come out."

Pen had watched Hoffman and his fiancée's interaction with Anna on his mind. He recalled Anna's lovely face and her soft voice—when she was not censuring him—and tenderness stoked his heart. But then worry began to creep in. The *Lexington Inn* being of higher quality than this abode did little to allay his fears and he had to remind himself that Anna had a Colt with her and she was not a person to be trifled with. And now she had Libby—who was just as spirited—to support her.

"My felicitations," he said to Alexander after Sophia had disappeared.

Hoffman's grin was wide, no doubt the happiness of a man in love. "Thank you. The wedding will be in Spring and I am extending the first invitation to you." He held out his hand and Pen automatically shook it. "Thank you for the warning. I will dress now and keep watch until morning."

Pen nodded. "Good. I must go after them now."

"Then I change my mind. I am coming with you. Allow me a minute to get into something appropriate and arrange for my man to watch the ladies instead."

Pen decided it would be worth having an extra person on his side, so he consented to wait. Hoffman reappeared shortly later, dressed rather haphazardly and holding a pistol. "Are you armed?"

"Yes."

They crossed the hall to the stairwell. "How did you come to know about this scheme?"

"One of them took my sister some days ago."

Hoffman stopped dead in his tracks, his expression horrified. "Tell me you've found her."

"I have."

"Where is she now?"

"At the *Lexington Inn* with Duchess Wrexford. Lady Anna helped me find and rescue Elizabeth."

"Good Lord," Hoffman said again. It seemed he was still somewhat in a state of shock. He clenched his jaw and gave Pen a determined look. "Let's make sure these scoundrels pay for this."

Pen gave him further details on their way down. Hoffman was the first to reach the bottom of the stairs and someone crashed into him. It was Julius Crispin. Hoffman was a stocky man and the force of the impact sent the duty manager tumbling to the floor.

"Sir, I saw him," Julius said in a loud whisper.

Hoffman eased from his defensive stance on seeing that Pen knew the man.

"Where?" Pen asked.

The manager struggled to his feet, panting. "He is in his chambers gathering his belongings. He plans to run."

With Julius leading them, they raced to Mr. Baker's room, and sure enough, found him throwing clothes into a valise. When he saw them, he stopped packing and made for the window. Oh no, you don't, Pen thought, and launched around the bed. He grabbed the man by his collar before tackling him to the ground.

Since tying people up was fast becoming second

nature to him, so to speak, he ordered the duty manager and Hoffman to find something with which to restrain Baker before dragging him to the bed and pulling him up into a sitting position beside a post. Pieces from a ripped shirt were handed over and he tied the man securely to the bedpost.

He stepped away to catch his breath as Hoffman asked, "Who are those involved in the plan to kidnap the ladies in my party?"

The man did not answer and Hoffman pulled out his pistol.

"Please don't shoot! I will tell you anything you want."

Just for the sake of it, Pen pulled out his revolver, too. "You'd better start talking, before one of us completely loses our patience."

The man started sobbing. "It was not my idea. It was Singer's. He was hired by a Sir Anthony to kidnap a lady in Boston and he discovered he could kidnap young ladies and demand ransoms from their families."

"And you thought it would make you quick money, too, you greedy scum." Pen seethed. He did not think himself particularly quarrelsome, but people appeared to be bringing out the worst in him lately.

"We have aborted the plan, I swear!"

"Who released Singer and Lily?" Pen asked.

"It was me. I heard them calling when I entered the bar—"

"Don't ramble. Just answer the question." Hoffman cut him off. "Where are they now?"

"I don't know. Once I heard we'd been found out I just wanted to leave."

"So you were going to abandon this place?" Pen asked.

Baker shook his head. "I was going to return later, after things calmed down."

Pen shrugged. "Well, you are not going anywhere now." Then he said to Hoffman, "Will you watch him while I search the building?"

"I'll watch him," Hoffman confirmed.

A SWEEP OF ALL ACCESSIBLE ROOMS IN THE INN yielded nothing. Pen confirmed that James had found the maid and delivered her as directed to Anna. On his man's return, they all waited in Baker's room until it was light enough to send James out to fetch the police. When they arrived, Pen explained in detail what had happened and had to admit to a huge sense of relief when first Baker, and then the minister Anders, were arrested. The remaining thugs and the mysterious Sir Anthony still needed to be tracked down. The task was not beyond the police here in Lexington, but Pen felt the Boston Police Department might be marginally more capable. He couldn't wait to collect Anna and his sister and return home.

"I cannot thank you enough, Penforth," Hoffman said as they watched the criminals taken away.

"Don't mention it."

"Please give my best to Lady Elizabeth and Lady Anna."

"I will."

The whole situation had seemed like it would never end, but victory was finally theirs. Pen could now take his beloved and sister home. After providing Julius with a hefty reward for his help he mounted his horse and began the short journey back to the *Lexington Inn.*

It was fortunate that he was not riding fast because, as he approached a small house along the road, he watched a man attaching a satchel to the saddle of a horse. There was something about the man's manner that hinted at furtive. Pen couldn't put his finger on it, but his attention stayed on the man rather than glancing and dismissing as one would normally do. The man had blonde hair and a wide-brimmed hat that obscured his face, until he looked up and caught sight of Pen.

Their eyes met and he saw recognition flare in the man's face. Was this the mysterious Sir Anthony? Just as Pen shifted direction and started to head toward him, the man launched himself onto his horse and whipped it into motion.

Damn it! Pen chased him at full speed. His blood rushed, carrying the resolve to take down Sir Anthony Hart all the way through his body. He rode hard and fast, and his opponent did just the same. Pen started to gain some ground, until Sir Anthony pulled out a gun and wildly fired a shot at his pursuer.

Pen grinned. Since everyone seemed to be going mad, he decided to join in the madness and pulled out his own firearm. He thought a warning shot might slow the man down or even deter him from shooting again, but it did not. Another loud blast that barely missed Pen's ear caused his mount to suddenly rear up and almost unseat him.

He maintained his tight grasp on the reins and gripped his legs against the horse's body until it returned to four legs and began to calm. They were no longer moving. Sir Anthony quickly disappeared into the fog ahead. Whatever Pen did, he could not convince the horse to move while still on its back, so eventually he dismounted and walked it instead. By the time he reached the inn housing his loved ones, his bad leg hurt. A lot.

THE INN WAS ALREADY ABUZZ WITH EARLY MORNING activity when Pen arrived and he went straight to Anna and Libby's room.

He heard Anna's voice asking who it was.

"It's me, Anna. Let me in."

The door flew open and she flung herself into his arms. He held her tightly. She was trembling.

"What is it?" He pulled away to look into her eyes.

"I was so worried."

"For me?" A smile curved his lips and he pulled her back to him, cradling her head under his chin. "I am fine. The police have taken over now. Several of the perpetrators are now in custody."

"Thank God!" She looked up at him, with relief in her eyes. But the worry was still there, etched in her brows and around her mouth. "There is something you should see." She led him into the room.

Libby slid off the bed when he entered and

handed him a paper from the vanity table. He read the words carefully: *I am not finished with you!*

"Not long after you left, this was slipped under the door."

"It is in Sir Anthony's hand," Libby confirmed.

"I saw him," Pen said grimly, recalling his failed chase.

"He's been captured?" Anna asked hopefully.

"Unfortunately not. He shot at me and scared my horse. There was no catching him. But I will see that the police track him down. And *this* threat?" He began ripping the paper. "No harm is going to come to either of you again. I promise."

Libby hugged him and Anna joined. Out of the corner of his eye, he noticed Marguerite sitting in one of the chairs by the fireplace. He gave her a nod of acknowledgment and she blushed.

He asked for food to be brought up to the room and after they had all eaten, they got into the Armstrong-Leeds carriage and began the journey home. Libby and Marguerite sat on the front-facing seat while he and Anna shared the one opposite. He didn't want her far from him. Not anymore. Once the carriage began moving, he leaned back and closed his eyes, finding some peace for the first time in nearly a week. Exhaustion settled in and he finally gave into it.

CHAPTER SEVENTEEN

Sometimes life went by with ease and placidity, and sometimes it served hardship after hardship. Instead of giving the Armstrong-Leeds and the Trevallyn families a moment of reprieve after the anguish they had endured, it sent a scandal their way, and it did so with merry satisfaction.

The scene that welcomed them as the carriage rolled to a stop in front of the Armstrong-Leeds house almost sent Anna into shock. There was a huge crowd gathered; gossipy aristocrats, curious passersby, and vulture-like reporters.

She was certain that right now there was nothing quite as diverting as the story they were after. And until a bigger story came out, this was their life now.

A man pointed to their carriage—it was rather unmistakable with the family crest emblazoned so boldly—and cried, "They have returned!" The mob surrounded the carriage, yelling at the top of their lungs.

Libby buried her face in her hands while Marguerite's eyes widened with fear. Not the best first impression of Boston, Anna supposed. Pen cursed under his breath and pushed his head through the window.

"Get away! Move!" He shouted over the din.

Anna pulled him back inside. He could get hurt. He rapped on the carriage roof, but the driver could not move, at least not without running someone over.

"What are we going to do?" Anna asked, trying to keep calm. She reached forward and gave Libby's shoulder a comforting squeeze.

"Let us wait for a bit," Pen suggested. "Someone will be out to clear the way in a moment, I am sure."

Fortunately, he was correct. Anna snuck a peek out the curtained window and watched as a small army of footmen emerged from the side of the house carrying hunting rifles. Like magic, the crowd dispersed somewhat, allowing the footmen to clear a path leading up to the front door of Pen and Libby's Boston home.

They alighted quickly, Anna throwing a protective arm over the young maid who was trembling. As they marched up the steps and into the house, the crowd surged back, ad questions were thrown at them from every which way.

"Is it true that Lady Elizabeth eloped?"

"Can we get an interview for *The Brahmin Times*?"

"Is she married now?"

"Who is the husband?"

"Was she kidnapped?"

Libby covered her ears and ran, and Anna ushered Marguerite inside as quickly as she could.

Finally, they were safe within the walls of the house where the raucous crowd couldn't reach them. Christiana came running into the hall with her arms open wide. Anna had never seen a happier mother.

"Libby! Oh, Libby!" She took her daughter into her arms and peppered Libby's face with kisses. "My darling girl!" She was crying now and Mary joined them, also hugging and crying. Anna felt her eyes pooling too so she looked away.

Pen's hand found hers and he leaned close and

whispered, "We did well, did we not? We make a good team."

She grinned. It was the first time he'd acknowledged her as being his equal and it delighted her no end.

"Pen, Anna," Christiana interrupted her musing. "Thank you for bringing her home to me." Then she embraced them one after the other.

Pen turned to Anna. "Get yourself settled. I am going to take care of the drama outside."

"All right."

She was so exhausted every part of her body ached, but it appeared as though her exhaustion was nowhere near as deep as his. His limp was more pronounced, his jaw was shadowed with stubble and the left side of his face where Singer had hit him was purple with bruising. But he looked happy. That stern brooding countenance was somehow more approachable.

Perhaps *she* had done that, or partly so. It would be splendid indeed if she had contributed to his newfound happiness. He had certainly created a bloom of new feeling within her own heart.

"Ma'am?" Someone called her.

She turned to find Marguerite wringing her hands and looking lost.

"Oh, Marguerite! Forgive me."

The girl smiled tremulously. "It is all right. I..." She stopped suddenly and shrugged, and Anna realized she was lost as to what to do or where to go now that she was in Boston.

The other ladies had disappeared upstairs already, so Anna motioned for Antoine.

"What do you want to do?" Anna asked the girl.

She smiled shyly. "I was hoping I could be in your employ, ma'am."

She wanted security, poor thing.

"Of course, you can stay with me as long as you wish. This is not my house, however. I live just a short distance away and when the crowd clears we can go there. In the meantime..."

She gestured to Antoine who had been waiting for her instruction. "This is Marguerite. In the future she will be in my employ, but for today she is a friend. Please see that she's taken care of while we're here."

He bowed to Anna. "As you wish, Your Grace."

AFTER A HOT BATH AND A DELICIOUS LUNCH, ANNA felt much better. She borrowed a dress of cream and green from Libby and dressed herself, for once deciding to ditch a corset entirely. She was not in the mood to suffer any constraint.

"Anna," Libby called from the bed where she was rearranging the pillows behind her to make them more comfortable.

"Yes?" Anna looked up from tying the laces of her boots.

"You and Pen…"

Anna smiled at her friend, feeling her cheeks warming.

"When did it happen?" Libby's eyes gleamed, and Anna realized immediately that she had her friend's blessing.

"It happened while we were searching for you. When we finally acknowledged our feelings, however, we realized that we've wanted each other for a long time, but have both been too foolish and stubborn to admit it."

Libby burst into delighted laughter. "That is so like you and Pen. You are both too headstrong for your own good. It will be an interesting match, to say the least."

"I love him," Anna admitted, sitting beside Libby on the bed.

She was folded into a prolonged sisterly embrace. Finally, Libby let her go and said, "I am sure he loves you, too." She pulled away then and gave Anna a funny look. "I knew something was up with him. Did you know, he has *never* missed any of your social events."

"Honestly, I didn't realize that until he mentioned it."

Libby's eyes took on a dreamy cast. "This is so romantic."

Anna nodded, feeling her cheeks grow even warmer than before.

"All our talk about never getting married," she began, then stopped, appalled. "Oh, Libby, I didn't mean—"

"It's fine," Libby assured her. "Pen will help ensure the annulment, and then…sisters for real!"

Anna chuckled self-consciously. "He hasn't actually asked, yet."

Libby smacked her gently on the arm. "Of course, he will! And I hope you'll say yes when he does!"

"I wouldn't have admitted my feelings to him otherwise."

"You're right." Libby jumped out of bed. "I have to tell Mama."

"Oh, wait!" Before Anna could stop her, she'd run out of the room, shouting, "Pen wants to marry Anna!"

Moments later Mary burst in and ran up to

Anna for a hug. "I have been waiting for this for so long. I'm so excited that Pen will officially make you part of our family."

Anna couldn't speak due to the emotion constricting her throat. Their acceptance of her was heartwarming.

LEAVING LIBBY AND MARY TO REST AFTER THE celebration of her courtship with Pen, Anna went downstairs, unsure what to do with herself. Sleep was an option as she was truly in want of it, but she was too restless to allow it quite yet.

When she reached the grand foyer, she peeped out and realized there was not a single soul in front of the house. How had Pen managed to clear the rabble? It was very impressive, to say the least. He knew how to command people to do what he wanted and he never took the charming route when doing so. She found it fascinating and intensely attractive.

Peering again through the window, she saw Edith Harper strutting up the steps. Anna smoothed her hands over her dress and opened the door before the hateful woman could even knock.

The riot that had greeted them on arrival had

so disoriented her that she'd not had the chance to think about who might have spread the story of Libby's disappearance around town.

But now it seemed the perpetrator had brought herself along to gloat.

"Oh!" Edith squealed in surprise, then recovered and looked Anna over. "My, you look…rough."

Anna ignored her taunt and simply remained blocking the doorway, disinclined to allow her in.

"I heard Lady Elizabeth had returned and I came to check on her," Edith said, adjusting her gloves.

Anna smiled grimly. "She's perfectly fine."

Edith curled her lip and gave Anna a reproachful look.

"Why did you do it, Edith?"

The woman shrugged. "The terms of the agreement the prince had me sign were impossible to meet. Finding her was taking too long. I am sure he set those terms so I could never get the money."

"How is keeping quiet impossible? Were you so desperate?"

Edith's eyes turned resentful and she said through clenched teeth, "I sold the story to the highest bidder. *The Brahmin Times* paid quite well."

"Of course they did. We'll see how long it will last."

That jab had been carefully aimed and it hit Edith perfectly. Hinting at her brother's gambling debt was probably a low blow and Anna felt bad resorting to pettiness, but she'd been pushed. Edith had chosen to blackmail and betray them.

"You are a truly horrible person, Anna."

"At least I know what loyalty means."

Edith's mouth fell open and Anna took the opportunity to shut the door in her face.

She leaned against the paneled wood for a couple of minutes to recover her equilibrium, before straightening and turning. She was about to enter one of the drawing rooms when the front door reopened and Pen walked in, this time accompanied by Mr. Graves and two other police officers.

Pen had obviously bathed too. He looked clean and far more rested. He was dressed in an afternoon coat of deep blue. Anna decided he looked handsome beyond belief. Seeing him made the unpleasantness of Edith Harper's visit drift away to nothing.

She accompanied the gentlemen into the drawing room and she and Pen took it in turns to explain everything that had happened since the last time they had seen Mr. Graves. As Libby was resting, the officers decided to return on the morrow for her statement. Anna and Pen were left alone after the police departed and he moved to sit beside her on the sofa.

"How are you, Anna?" He took her hands in his.

She smiled up at him. "I am fine now that I know those men will be hunted down and captured."

He pulled her close. "Me too."

She snuggled in to him, basking in his warmth and breathing in his delightful scent—sandalwood and mint.

"Anna," he said eventually.

"Yes?"

"Did you go back to your room at the *Five Castles* when I went down to the public area to look for Singer?"

Oh, dear! She shook her head, and he sighed loudly.

"How did you know?" she asked carefully.

"You mentioned you'd found the list of names in Singer's bedroom. It didn't register at the time, but I've since understood what you must have done."

She avoided his eyes when she said, "That was somewhat careless of me."

He tucked a finger under her chin and lifted her face so he could look into her eyes. "I want you to be more careful in future. That was dangerous."

He was right, of course. She could not imagine what would have happened if she had been discovered underneath the bed.

"You mean more to me than you will ever know," Pen added.

He meant more to her, too. "I will be careful. I promise."

He burst into laughter. She frowned, wondering what had gotten to him. "I can't believe you didn't argue with me about that," he said.

Now she laughed too. "I suppose I must have grown."

"So have I," he admitted, stroking her cheek. "And you helped with that."

She closed her eyes briefly to better enjoy the warm happy feeling that was circling her.

He cradled her face in his hands then. "You saved my life, and I don't mean just what you did at the bar. I was on a path to self-destruction, shutting out those who matter the most to me, and you brought me back from that. You saved me from myself."

"Pen—"

He pressed his lips to hers. She had to admit, it was an effective way to silence her.

Eventually he pulled back. "There's more."

"Really? Do go on. I'm enjoying this." She grinned happily up at him, enjoying the softness in his features.

"Anna, you made me aware of the reason you fight for women's rights, and I feel ashamed for trivializing that battle. You have my irrevocable support and please know that I consider you my equal."

Her heart skipped a beat at his words. His thumbs moved over her cheeks to wipe away tears she didn't even realize had fallen.

"Even in a fistfight, you're my equal. And in a gunfight, you are my superior."

She laughed. "I can't believe you're admitting this."

"Well, believe it because it is true. It is one of the truest things I feel."

"Oh, Pen…" She didn't even know what to say. There was so much emotion swirling around inside her.

"I love you, Anna Trevallyn." His eyes bored deep into hers and she read the truth there.

"And I love you, Penforth. With all my heart."

"Good," he said, straightening. "You shouldn't have a problem marrying me now." When she started to speak, he silenced her again, this time with a finger against her lips. "We have to marry. We've posed as a couple so many times already. So what do you say? When do we get married?"

She shook her head, feigning affront. "You're impossibly controlling."

A sheepish smile touched his features. "Oh, I was supposed to ask you first, wasn't I?"

She leaned back and folded her arms across her chest.

He bolted from the chair saying, "Wait here. I'll be right back," and hurried out of the room. Moments later, he returned and slowly, struggling because of his leg injury, he knelt before her. He presented her with a ring, a beautiful cabochon diamond with a delightful sapphire on either side.

"Family heirloom," he said, when her eyebrows raised upward. "And this one reminds me of your eyes. Sapphires are darker than your eyes obviously, but—"

"Are you going to ask me or not?"

He sucked in a breath and let it out slowly. "Lady Anna Trevallyn, will you make me the happiest man alive by accepting my hand in marriage?"

"Yes, Penforth, I will."

He slid the ring onto her finger and then she assisted him up from the floor. Once they were seated, he pulled her into a sweet slow kiss. Every corner of her heart was filled with joy. She was a fortunate woman and she was thankful for her good fortune. Although she could no longer deny the existence of luck, she rather thought it was providence.

"Anna," he said into her hair.

"Yes?"

"You will stay here until your mother returns, won't you?"

"Hmm. I might. Or I might not."

"You minx."

She grinned against his chest, snuggling close, and he held her tight.

Several days later

The criminals were caught, all except Sir Anthony Hart, but the hunt for him continued. Anna and Pen shared the news of their engagement to everyone's delight, especially Libby who already considered Anna her sister.

Penforth was a different man. He tolerated Treacle more, and was even caught by Mary stroking the animal in his study by the fireplace just hours after he'd shocked Antoine by whistling as he walked down the hall.

Life truly couldn't get any better…but it could get worse.

Anna was in the drawing room perusing a bridal magazine with Libby while Pen attended to business in his study when the police arrived.

"Sir."

Pen looked up from the document he was reading and gave Antoine a beleaguered look. "I thought I asked not to be disturbed."

"Pardon me, Sir. Mr. Graves is here, and he says it is urgent."

"Hmm." Hopefully, he brought news of Sir Anthony's capture. "Send him in."

"I have already shown him to the small salon. He asked to see her ladyship."

Pen raised a brow at his butler. There were four ladies in the house.

"Lady Elizabeth," he clarified.

With a sigh, he pushed back his chair and stood. He met Libby and Anna on their way to the salon and they proceeded together. Mr. Graves was standing when they entered. He had come alone this time.

"Has he been found?" Pen asked without any greeting. He felt it was unnecessary.

Mr. Graves wore an odd expression, from which Pen was unable to discern meaning. "A *body* has been found," the policeman said slowly.

Pen frowned while Anna sucked in her breath.

"Yesterday, we discovered a body in a ditch just outside of Boston. It was identified to be a Mr. Nolan Hart."

Pen was confused. "Nolan?"

"Yes," Graves replied. "Mr. Nolan Anthony Hart."

A tiny gasp erupted from Anna, but Libby was silent.

"How did he die?" Pen asked.

This was it. The last criminal had been captured, albeit not alive, but at least the nightmare was truly over now.

"Multiple stab wounds to the body as well as trauma to the head."

Anna winced. Libby remained expressionless.

"He was murdered then."

"Indeed." The policeman turned to Libby, pulling out a small book and a ball pen. "I would like to ask you a few questions, Lady Elizabeth, if you don't mind."

She nodded slowly, seeming a little dazed. "Go on," she said at last.

"Records show that you are married to this man. What can you confirm about this marriage?"

"It was a forced marriage. I was threatened and I thought I had no choice."

"Pardon the crassness of my next question. Has

this marriage been…err…consummated in any way?"

Libby's cheeks turned pink. "No, it has not. I was held captive throughout until my rescue from that crypt under the church."

Graves glanced at Pen then and a strange feeling began to settle around his heart. It felt like dread.

"Is there any action being taken against this marriage?" Graves queried.

Pen answered this time. "Yes, an annulment has already been filed."

The policeman finished scrawling in his notebook and tucked it away in his coat before addressing Libby. "Princess Elizabeth Armstrong-Leeds, Baroness of Esk, I regret to inform you that you are the primary suspect in the murder of your husband, Mr. Nolan Anthony Hart."

The End

Libby's story continues in *Not Quite a Baroness*
The Boston Heiresses (Book 2)

Then read on for Lady Sarah's story in *Not Quite a Lady*

The Boston Heiresses (Book 3)

ABOUT THE AUTHOR

Ava Rose writes sweet and clean Victorian historical romance and gothic mystery. Her heroines are feisty and independent and her heroes brooding and swoon-worthy. When she's not writing, Ava looks after the family, pampers various cats, and tries to find a smidgen of time for her husband. She lives in Melbourne, Australia.

www.ingramcontent.com/pod-product-compliance
Lightning Source LLC
Chambersburg PA
CBHW020132120726

47903CB00007B/2223

9780648404521